"Are you suggesting I'm a cheap gold digger?"

Lesley's temper was skyrocketing.

"Well, aren't you?" Zack retorted. "Money seemed to have been the crux of our problems when we were married. I can't see you taking on another poor man."

"Money had nothing to do with why I divorced you," Lesley cried heatedly.

"Didn't it?" he jeered.

Lesley jumped to her feet, her eyes blazing. "No, it didn't." At his sneer of disbelief, she lost all restraint, shouting, "Tell me, what happened to your leg? Some bull did that to you, didn't it? I knew that it would happen some day, that or you'd be killed. Well, I couldn't take waiting for it to happen anymore!"

He seemed stunned by her impassioned outburst, and his face lost color. She picked up his jacket and held it out to him. "Goodbye, Zack."

SANDRA K. RHOADES began reading romance novels for relaxation when she was studying for her engineering degree and became completely hooked. She was amazed at how much fun the books are, and before long her sights were set on a career in romance writing. Colorado-born, she now lives in British Columbia with her husband and their two children. There she raises livestock, and every summer keeps a large garden.

Books by SANDRA K. RHOADES

HARLEQUIN PRESENTS
917—A RISKY BUSINESS
956—BITTER LEGACY
1021—SHADOWS IN THE LIMELIGHT

SANDRA K. RHOADES

yesterday's embers

Harlequin Books

TORONTO • NEW YORK • LONDON
AMSTERDAM • PARIS • SYDNEY • HAMBURG
STOCKHOLM • ATHENS • TOKYO • MILAN

To my daughters,
Brandy and Leslie,
for all their help
and encouragement.
Love Mom.

Harlequin Presents first edition October 1989
ISBN 0-373-11214-9

Original hardcover edition published in 1989
by Mills & Boon Limited

CHAPTER ONE

DEAR DADDY.

How are you? I am fine. School's OK. I'll be glad when summer vacation starts. I'll have to stay with Mrs Sheppard while Mom's at work. She's here tonight because Mom's out with Brian. I wish I didn't have to have a babysitter. I'm going to be eleven next week and am too old to be treated like a little kid. I was hoping Mom would buy me a bigger horse for my birthday. I don't think she will. She's going to let me have a sleep-over. I have to go do my homework now.

Love, Mandy.

P.S. XOXOXOXOXOXOXOXO

'Here's your drink.'

Zack Mackenzic didn't look up as he accepted the bourbon but continued to frown down at the sheet of notepaper in his hand. He was a big man, lean and rangy, an outdoor man who looked incongruous against the impersonal elegance of the apartment. His long legs, encased in tight denims, jutted out into the room as he lay sprawled in the chair. The hands holding the paper were hard and calloused, his rugged, sun-bronzed features grim as he contemplated the letter from his daughter.

'So how was Houston?' his companion prompted.

He looked up and shrugged. 'Fine. The opening for the new outlet went well, we even had some of the cast from *Dallas* there.'

He fell silent, forgetting his companion once again. However, she persisted, 'Did you get your picture taken with a movie star?' Dragging his attention back to Betsy Turner, Zack grimaced, then shook his head. He'd been spared that. While he was proud of his achievements as a professional rodeo rider, and after his retirement his success as a businessman, he'd never enjoyed the personal publicity that accompanied his career choices. He didn't enjoy the limelight, even on the arm of a Hollywood starlet.

'No, I managed to avoid the flashbulbs. By the way, thanks for picking me up from the airport.' Involuntarily he glanced back at the letter that had been awaiting his return and once again lasped into a morose silence.

Betsy gave him a speculative look and, not being above a broad hint, asked, 'What's Mandy got to say . . . bad news?'

Zack's mouth twisted wrily. 'No, not really . . . although I had forgotten her birthday is in a few days. I'll have to send something off pretty quick if it's to get there in time.' He held the letter out to her. 'You want to read it?'

'Sure.' Betsy accepted the note from her goddaughter and Zack settled back into his chair with his thoughts as she read. He felt badly about forgetting Mandy's birthday. He wasn't much of a father to her as it was, only seeing her a couple of times a year. The least he could do was make sure she knew she was in his thoughts even when he wasn't with her, especially on special days like her birthday.

He'd missed her birth, and sometimes he

wondered if his absence then hadn't been an omen for the future. He'd been looking forward to his child's arrival, a little fearfully, but eagerly too. He and Lesley had pored over books on natural childbirth, and she'd practised breathing techniques for labour for hours while he'd coached her.

As it turned out, though, when Lesley went into labour he hadn't even been around. He'd had a rodeo that day, and had won his calf-roping event. His best friend, Jerry Turner, Betsy's late husband, had won his bull-riding event as well. As the baby wasn't even due for a month, he hadn't even stopped to consider when Jerry and a bunch of the others invited him along on a pub crawl.

By the time Betsy had found him and Jerry to tell them Lesley had gone to the hospital, they were both three sheets to the wind. His wife had been tight-lipped and furious when he'd finally got to her. He supposed he couldn't blame her. The bouquet of red roses he'd brought couldn't mask the stink of whisky. More importantly, his daughter had been born and he'd missed it. It didn't seem to matter much at that point that he had planned to make that rodeo his last until after the birth, just so he could be with Lesley when the time came. The facts were that he was at a rodeo when Lesley had gone into labour, was out getting drunk when she had needed his support.

Premature, Mandy had been delicate at first, so when Lesley got out of the hospital she'd taken her back to her parents' farm in Colorado. If he hadn't felt so guilty, he might not have let her. Her parents had never had much time for him, and he returned their animosity. He hadn't thought they would succeed in turning her totally against him, though.

Even when Mandy was stronger and Lesley still wouldn't rejoin them on the rodeo circuit, he wouldn't admit that was what was happening. He'd known she'd wanted him to settle down, give up the rodeo and live the dull, narrow life her parents did. He couldn't do that, though, even for her. Maybe because he'd never really believed she'd end it between them if he didn't. Until she'd divorced him five years ago, he'd still held out hope they'd make a go of it some day.

He hadn't seen her since. He'd kept contact with Mandy, having her stay with him a couple of times a year. However, he wouldn't go out to the farm, not even after her parents had died in a road accident.

Her folks had hated cowboys and horses, he mused, his thoughts moving at a tangent. 'Lesley ought to get Mandy a decent mount,' Zack said suddenly. 'She can't expect her to ride that little Shetland for the rest of her life.'

Finished with the letter, Betsy set it aside. 'Oh, she probably has her reasons,' she placated, and Zack gave her an impatient look. For once, he wished she would come down on his side, but from experience, he should know she'd sit on the fence whenever it came to a discussion of his ex-wife. She was still friends with Lesley, even if she was his friend as well. She always refused to take sides—even though she probably agreed with him!

Zack was still scowling as she said, 'Lesley probably doesn't have time to look after a big animal, what with her job and all.'

'Her job!' Zack snorted. 'She ought to be staying home looking after Mandy. For all her faults, I never thought she'd turn into one of those women's libber types, hankering after fulfilment,' he sneered.

'I doubt if she's finding fulfilment waiting tables,' Betsy said drily.

'Waiting tables? I thought she had a job at that new motel out on the interstate.'

'She does. She works in the coffee-shop.'

Zack's lips pressed together. 'I thought she was a receptionist or something. How come you never told me she was serving coffee?' he demanded.

'You never asked. Besides, what's wrong with being a waitress? The pay's not that bad, and she hasn't a lot of options open to her. After all, she married you before she had chance to finish high school.'

'It's damn hard work,' he muttered. He shifted uncomfortably. Lesley had only been seventeen when he'd married her. Maybe he shouldn't have rushed her into marriage until she was a little older and had finished her education. On the other hand, she'd been just as keen to tie the knot as he had, so he didn't have any reason to feel guilty. None the less his tone was defensive as he said, 'You must have it wrong. If she's waiting tables, it's not because she needs the money. Her old man would have left her a packet when he died. He never did let me forget that he was the wealthy farmer whose only daughter had taken up with a rodeo bum.'

Betsy winced at the bitterness of his tone. Roy Hammond had been dead for four years, but Zack still carried a grudge against him.

He nailed her with a hard stare. 'Has Lesley said anything to you about needing money? Maybe you're supposed to soften me up? Tell me, did she hear about Sheridan Inc. and decided she wants on the gravy train? Well, she threw my money back in my face five years ago, and I'm not giving her a second chance.'

'That was her dad's doing, and you know it. He was the one that didn't want you having anything to do with Mandy, didn't even want you to make support payments. As for Lesley saying anything about money now . . .' Betsy shook her head. 'She's never said a word. It's just I've noticed things. The place has really run down since her dad died, the car she drives . . . that kind of thing. I just don't think she's got a lot of money.'

'So what am I suppose to do about it? Offer her alimony now?'

Betsy shrugged, and reached over to look at the letter again. 'Maybe she won't need it.'

'What do you mean by that?'

She gestured with the letter. 'This Brian . . . isn't that the same guy Mandy mentioned when she was here at Christmas? If he's been going out with Lesley that long, maybe it's serious. She could marry him.'

Zack's forehead creased with a frown. Somehow he had never thought about Lesley getting married again—although he supposed there wasn't any reason he shouldn't have. She was only twenty-nine and, unless she'd changed radically in the last five years, she must still be an attractive woman, beautiful even. She'd been pretty when he married her, with the promise of real beauty when she matured. It was only logical that she would re-marry someday—but this Brian fellow . . .?

'Mandy said she couldn't stand him. Lesley surely wouldn't marry some guy Mandy didn't get along with.'

Betsy shrugged non-committally. 'Maybe, maybe

not. Anyway, I'd best be moving on.' She stood up to take her leave, and Zack followed her to his feet. 'Are you going to be in town for a while now that the Houston trip is over?'

'Yes, I expect so.' He hesitated. 'I might take some time off, though. Maybe I'll see if I can have Mandy come stay for a few days. I should have had her at Easter, but then this trip intervened.'

'And have her miss school? It won't be out for another month.'

'I hadn't thought about that,' he admitted, running his hand through his dark hair. 'Well, I do want to see her, so I'll figure something out.'

As he made a move to accompany her to the door, she waved him away and he felt a twinge of annoyance. He didn't need pampering. The plane ride had caused his bad leg to stiffen so that his uneven gait was more pronounced than usual, but he could still walk with her to the door. The leg had been crushed under an irate Brahma bull a couple of years ago when the animal had fallen. Ironically, he had never been keen on bullriding, only participating in it because he needed a riding sport to combine with his calf-roping speciality to qualify for All-round Cowboy.

However, the accident and resulting injury had ended his roping career. In calf-roping, the cowboy rides his horse hard after the calf, roping him with a lariat that has one end tied to the saddle horn. When the calf is caught, the cowboy dismounts and runs to the calf while his horse keeps the rope taut. He throws the animal to the ground and ties three of its legs together with a rawhide strip called a piggin' string. As a timed event, every fraction of a second counts from the moment the calf breaks the barrier to when the cowboy raises his hands to signal that it's tied. With his game leg, Zack was too slow for professional competition, where times of under ten seconds were common. Although his injury wouldn't have interfered with his continuing as a bullrider, Zack had decided to retire.

Ignoring Betsy's protest, Zack moved with her to the door and held it open for her. When he'd closed it behind her, he leaned briefly against the solid barrier, staring thoughtfully into space. It had been years since he'd been with his daughter on her birthday . . .

Lesley was just sliding the macaroni and cheese casserole into the oven when she heard She-Ra bark and the sound of a vehicle pulling into the yard. She closed the oven door, then leaned against the counter for a moment before going out to see who it was. It was probably John Murray. She'd noticed he had finished planting the lower twenty fields several days ago and had probably come by to pick up her cheque for the seed he'd used.

John had been renting the fields from her ever since her dad had died. Farm commodity prices being what they were, she didn't make a lot of money on the arrangement, but the cheque she got each autumn for her share of the crops made the mortgage payment on the farm with a little left over.

However, it was standard in these arrangements for the owner to share the cost of spring seed and fertilizer. John would have paid for the seed, and consequently needed her share of the planting costs to pay off the debt. Although Lesley had the money in the bank, it was depressing to think about writing out the cheque. While she was a good manager, every dime in her account seemed to have somewhere important to go. Just once, it would be nice to spend money on something fun, like an extravagant new outfit or a super surprise for Mandy. One got so tired of just paying the bills.

The dog had quietened by the time Lesley glanced over to the clock and saw she been procrastinating for over ten minutes. Mandy was outside doing her chores, so she supposed her daughter had been entertaining John in the interim. However, an almost eleven-year-old couldn't keep him occupied indefinitely, especially as he probably just wanted his money so he could go home for his supper. She found her purse and, taking out her cheque-book, slipped it into the back pocket of her jeans before going out to see him.

However, it wasn't John's battered old green Dodge pick-up she saw parked over by the barn when she came out of the house. This vehicle was far more impressive. It was a big three-quarter ton pick-up fitted with a matching camper and towing a double horse-trailer. It looked practically brand new with its silver and charcoal paintwork gleaming in the late afternoon sunshine.

There didn't seem to be a soul around and, frowning slightly, Lesley advanced towards the vehicle. She felt the faintest niggling of apprehension when she saw the orange and black Wyoming plates, but even that didn't prepare her for the words scrawled in silver against the dark grey of the driver's side door.

Zack Mackenzie—World Champion All-Around Cowboy.

For one stunned instant she froze, a swift dart of

pain flashing through her chest. She recovered a moment later, shaking her head slightly as her heart settled back into its normal rhythm. Betsy must have borrowed Zack's truck. She knew he lived in Cheyenne and, for the odds that he would ever come here, that might as well be a million miles away.

Having reached that conclusion, her poor heart came in for another jolt when the barn door suddenly opened and her daughter darted out, followed more slowly by her ex-husband.

'Mom! Look who's here!' Mandy shouted, bounding up to her.

Lesley didn't need the injunction. Her eyes were so firmly riveted to the figure now lounging against the door-jamb of the barn, she didn't think she'd ever be able to tear them away. He didn't seem to have changed a bit in the five years since she'd last seen him. His physical appeal still beckoned, even after all this time. For all their marital problems, sex had never been one of them. Forgotten nights where she had lain wrapped within his sinewed arms were suddenly crystal clear in her mind, drying her throat and setting off a host of unwanted sensations. His body was hard and lean, without an ounce of excess flesh; his face, sun-weathered and craggy; his eyes, black and unreadable.

Silent tension stretched between them as they stared at one another. When Mandy grabbed her hand and started tugging her towards Zack, Lesley finally remembered their audience. Taking a deep breath to pull herself together, she allowed her daughter to lead her up to him, even managing to summon a faint smile.

'Hello, Zack.' Her voice was almost normal.

'Lesley.' He tipped his hat to her, straightening

from his casual position against the jamb as he did so.

The action brought him closer and, involuntarily, Lesley took a half-step backwards. As she saw his brows quirk mockingly, she hastily looked away, her gaze coming to rest on her daughter. Mandy's eyes were moving between them like a spectator's at a tennis match, a faintly crest-fallen expression settling on her childish features.

It was Zack who remarked on it. 'Why the long face, Sweet-knees? Aren't you glad to see me?' Grinning down at her, he reached out to ruffle her hair.

Mandy looked down at the ground, digging a small hole in the sand with the toe of her shoe. 'I thought maybe . . .' The rest of the sentence was an unintelligible mumble.

Lesley cast her former husband an apologetic glance. Since Mandy had been fitted with braces, she tended to slur her words. On this occasion, though, she was secretly grateful for the impediment that got them past that first awkward moment and was diverting Zack's attention from herself. 'You'll have to speak clearer than that, honey,' Lesley reminded her daughter.

The child looked up and said all too clearly, 'I had thought maybe you and Daddy would kiss each other hello.'

Lesley's eyes widened in horrified dismay, as heat washed up her cheeks from her neck. Not for diamonds could she force herself to look over to Zack to find out his reaction to his daughter's tactlessness.

'Do you think we should?' she heard him ask. 'We're not married any more, you know.'

'But you're friends, aren't you? Mom always kisses her friend Brian, and they aren't married.'

Lesley was suddenly highly suspicious of her ingenuous child. She should have had the dentist weld the kid's jaw shut while he was at it! Mandy wasn't a gauche five-year-old, to be blurting out imprudent remarks. No, her daughter was a little-too-mature-for-her-age eleven—with a hitherto unsuspected matchmaking streak.

'Maybe you've got a point there,' Zack acknowledged, and Lesley's head jerked around to stare at him. Surely he wasn't going to play along with Mandy? However, she didn't like the look in those dark eyes of his now—it was all too readable.

When he stepped forward, she choked out, 'No, Zack.' It came out as a whisper, and before she could repeat it more loudly he'd hauled her to him, crushing her unwilling form against his hard chest and covering her mouth with his.

Oh, she fought him. Her palms against his shoulders, she pushed against him as hard as she could, but to no avail. Then, suddenly, she was fighting herself. Those long-dormant feelings, disturbed by that first sight of him, sprang fully alive at his touch, stampeding through her and trampling her resistance.

Sensing the change in her, his hold softened, his hands gently caressing her spine as his lips moved searchingly over hers. Her mouth parted to give access to its sweet inner softness, and his tongue probed to explore the smooth ivory of her teeth. Lesley's senses were whirling, reason spun out of existence by passion.

Disappointment stabbed through her like a sharp knife as his hands moved to her waist and gently pushed her back from him. Dazed, she stared up into his face, at those firm, sensuous lips that had destroyed all her inhibitions. They moved into a smile and he chuckled softly.

Then he looked away. 'Happier now?'

Her goggle-eyed daughter was grinning up at them, nodding vigorously. 'Wow, Dad, that was better than the movies!'

The lingering mists of desire vanished instantly. Movies! That kiss had been X-rated! How dared he? How dared he kiss her like that in front of Mandy? How dared he kiss her like that. Even her acute embarrassment at the idea of her child's having witnessed the scene failed beneath the onslaught of the fury that swept through her. It blocked her throat, stifling the words of outrage she wanted to fling at him, so that she could only glare at him in silent wrath.

And he had the nerve to grin back at her, his black eyes dancing with laughter! Before she could react with the swipe she wanted to take at him, he slipped his arm across Mandy's shoulders and turned away. 'Now that that's out of the way, come see your birthday present.'

Steaming, Lesley watched their retreat towards the rear of the horse-trailer. They'd only gone a few feet when she noticed the unevenness of his gait. He was limping.

The sight crippled her anger, causing it to fade. What had happened to him? In the years of their separation, she'd deliberately avoided seeking any news of him. Betsy, Mandy—they'd learned never to speak of Zack to her. A couple of years ago, Mandy had let slip he was no longer rodeoing, but Lesley had quickly changed the subject. Even her curiosity couldn't compel her to hear about him long enough to press for details. Zack was a subject that was simply too painful.

Had he quit because he'd been hurt? Ironically, that was one of the reasons she hadn't wanted to hear about him. She hadn't wanted to hear he was injured, lying somewhere in pain, or worse, killed by some rogue bull like Jerry Turner.

Now, though——Oh, God, how she wished they'd told her!

At the clatter of hooves, she moved, joining the other two at the rear of the rig. They already had the animal unloaded by the time she reached them, and were now admiring the Appaloosa mare. She was a beauty. Around fifteen hands, she was a rich, deep chestnut, with the spotted white blanket typical of the breed across her rump.

'What's her name?' Mandy asked.

'Oh, it's a mouthful, so why don't you just call her Sugar?' Zack replied. His hand rested lightly against the mare's withers, but his whole attention was on his daughter. She was staring at the horse in trancelike wonder—almost as though it were an apparition—and he couldn't help grinning. 'Aren't you going to make friends with her?'

'Oh, sure!' The spell broke and the girl moved to Sugar's head and ran her hand down the mare's white blaze. Her expression of rapt joy didn't alter. 'I can't believe she's really mine,' Mandy breathed.

'Believe it,' her father said. 'She's your birthday present.'

'Oh, thank you, Daddy!' Momentarily leaving the horse's head, Mandy threw herself at her father, clinging to his neck as he lifted her off her feet and hugged her.

Lesley watched the pair, her lower lip clamped hard between her teeth. An unworthy and thoroughly childish jealousy was gnawing at her. She'd known Mandy wanted a horse for her birthday— her daughter's hints weren't very subtle. She'd have liked to have got her one, too; however, there had just been no way she could see of managing it. Finances being what they were, some summer tops and shorts and a new bathing suit were a much more sensible—and affordable—gift. She didn't think her daughter was going to go into raptures over those, though. Even her 'frivolous' present of a new bridle for Mandy's Shetland, Toby, wasn't going to be much of a treat now that she had the Appaloosa mare.

Zack set her daughter back on her feet. 'So why don't you try her out? Her tack's up in the front of the trailer. I brought Clancy along to keep her company on the trip down and I'll go with you.'

'Super!' Mandy shot off around the side of the trailer, and Zack looked over to Lesley and saw her expression.

'You don't approve of my gift?'

Lesley wanted to say she didn't, wanted to pick a quarrel with him, but she knew it was only because she was jealous. So she made herself smile at him, saying, 'It's great, she loves it. She's been wanting a bigger horse for a long time.'

'But you weren't getting her one, were you?'

The way he said it, it sounded like he thought she denied the child out of simple perversity. Well, he could think what he liked. 'No, I wasn't going to get her one. I thought about it, but . . .' Lesley shrugged. Thinking about buying a horse had been all she could afford to do.

'Well, don't worry about it,' he advised sardonically. 'She won't be running off to the rodeos yet. She's a little young to be going on the rodeo circuit.'

He turned away and started to unlatch the trailer door so he could unload the other horse. Lesley stared at his back, hurt that he could so misinterpret her motives. Rodeoing had never even entered into it. Maybe she wouldn't be thrilled if Mandy decided to take it up when she was old enough, but she wouldn't stand in her way—or deny her a decent mount now because of that vague possibility in the future.

She had to step back out of the way when Zack's big quarter-horse gelding backed out of the trailer. To her surprise, she recognised the animal. When she'd heard the name 'Clancy' she'd thought he'd just named another horse that, but this was the same horse he'd used for calf-roping years ago.

She could still remember the bitter argument they'd had when Zack had bought him. She hadn't thought they could afford to pay out the kind of money his previous owner wanted for him, but Zack had insisted he needed a quality rope-horse if he was to succeed in his career.

She supposed Zack had been right—that *World Champion* sign on the side of his truck confirmed it. However, she hadn't wanted to admit it back then. She hadn't wanted to give in on anything that kept him following the rodeo.

As Zack tied the gelding to the rear of the trailer, Lesley walked over and stroked the animal's rump. She wanted to say something conciliatory, but only came up with, 'You kept him all this time.'

'That's right. I haven't used him for calf-roping

for years, but he's still a good horse, even if he is getting pretty long in the tooth.' His tone was stilted, and she knew he hadn't forgotten that long-ago quarrel either.

It was something of a relief to see Mandy coming back around the side of the trailer, hauling a western saddle. However, it didn't help Lesley's spirits any when she saw it was brand new, with her daughter's name tooled on the leather skirt. A matching bridle was looped over the horn, so any idea she might have conceived of trading in the pony bridle she got on a larger one to fit the new horse went out the window.

Zack went over to help Mandy saddle up. He was very good with his daughter, Lesley admitted: helping her and giving her advice, but not taking over like so many adults did when dealing with children. By the time she was up in the saddle, Mandy looked pretty proud of herself. No doubt about it, Sugar was the ideal gift for a horse-crazy eleven-year-old.

Lesley stayed where she was while Zack saddled Clancy. When they rode away, she started to walk back to the house and glanced over to see Toby standing in his paddock. The old pony trotted up the fence rail and neighed to the riders, but they didn't turn around. He stayed watching, though, until his mistress was out of sight, his soft brown eyes confused. Lesley knew just how he felt.

CHAPTER TWO

LESLEY gave herself a good talking to when she got back to the kitchen. It was time she started looking at this situation rationally. After all, she wasn't the only woman in the world to have an ex-husband, some of those actresses had dozens. She was a mature, civilised young woman of nearly thirty, and certainly capable of meeting her former husband with some degree of equanimity. For the past hour, her emotions had been roller-coastering up and down like a teenager's, and that wouldn't do. For Mandy's sake, she had to pull herself together and greet Zack with some sort of normality. She would have to put aside her possessiveness and jealousy and bury those old animosities, because, whatever happened, she couldn't let her child feel that her loyalties were being divided. The best way of assuring that would be to treat Zack as an old friend who'd come to call.

And an old friend would be invited to supper— though she couldn't serve him the macaroni and cheese. Aside from the fact that the casserole had dried to a leathery mess while she had been outside, she couldn't bring herself to serve that particular dish to Zack. In the early days of their marriage, they had practically lived on the stuff, only having meat when Zack won at the rodeo. Eating macaroni and cheese had become something of a standing joke.

So She-Ra, Mandy's collie, would dine on that tonight, and Lesley would have to figure out something else to serve. As much as she'd have liked to impress him with a nice juicy T-bone, steaks were an unknown commodity in her freezer. However, she could find a pound of mince to make up into Mexican food. *Burritos*—refried beans wrapped in *tortillas* and topped with a spicy meat and tomato sauce—were Mandy's favourite, and Lesley didn't fix it for her very often.

She'd spent a hectic hour and a half by the time Mandy and Zack got back from their ride. Though she was just using canned beans, there had still been the sauce to prepare, cheese to grate, lettuce and tomato to chop for garnish, and the big job, rolling out the tortillas.

However, she had it all ready and had even managed to do a quick run through the living-room with the vacuum. She'd also changed her jeans for a skirt and blouse, and pulled her long blonde hair back into a ponytail. While she might not look glamorous, at least she was neat by the time the other two walked in.

'When you've washed up, take your dad into the dining-room and I'll bring in supper,' Lesley enjoined as soon as her daughter came in. She could see from her expression that the child was still bubbling over with enthusiasm for the new horse, and dying to tell her about it. However, they'd never get down to the meal if Lesley let her start in before they sat down. As it was, supper was going to be served a couple of hours later than they usually ate it.

'OK,' Mandy accepted the order with equanimity. 'Come on, Dad, I'll show you where the bathroom is.'

As soon as they left, Lesley started dishing up the meal into serving dishes to take to the table. She had just finished when Zack came back into the room without his daughter.

'Anything I can do?' he offered.

'No, everything's ready. I just have to carry it in.' Despite her resolve to treat him like an old friend, she was still uncomfortable in his presence. She couldn't bring herself to look at him directly, and she quickly turned back to the counter to pick up the platter of *tortillas*. Her hand was shaking slightly, and she had to force herself to steady it before she could face him again.

'I didn't want to put you to any trouble. I could have taken Mandy out for dinner.'

'It's OK. She likes having you here . . . in her own home.' Damn, that sounded like an accusation and she hadn't meant it that way. Why did she have to be so nervous? She shot him a quick glance and was relieved to see he didn't seem to have noticed anything amiss in her remark.

'Well, at least let me help you carry things in.' He reached out and relieved her of the platter, and walked away with it to the dining-room. He was setting it down when she caught up with him.

'I wondered what you wanted to drink. Mandy and I usually have milk, but I've got some beer if you'd rather have that.'

'Beer would be fine. Or . . .' he hesitated '. . . I think I've got a bottle of wine in the camper. Would you share it with me if I brought it in?'

Instead of acting like old friends, they were conversing like two polite but wary strangers. She realised that he was as ill at ease as she was.

Somehow that made her feel better, and she was able to smile naturally at him for the first time since he'd arrived.

'Wine would be lovely. I'll bring in the rest of the meal while you fetch it.'

Lesley was just putting the finishing touches to the table when Mandy burst in a few minutes later. She'd scampered half-way into the room when she stopped and looked around her.

'Dad hasn't left, has he?' she asked in alarm.

'No, you know he wouldn't go without saying goodbye to you. He just went out to his truck to get a bottle of wine,' Lesley hastily reassured her.

Relaxing, Mandy approached the table. Lesley had got out her mother's good china and silver, and it sparkled elegantly in the light from the overhead lamp. 'Oh, Mom, this is just like a party. I wish we could eat in here every night and use the good dishes and everything. Can we have candles?'

Candlelight was too suggestive of a lovers' tête-à-tête, and Lesley was about to deny the request, when she caught a glimpse of her daughter's expectant face and capitulated. 'Sure, go ahead and get them out.' Dining with an exuberant eleven-year-old who would probably want to talk horses all through the meal was hardly likely to create a romantic atmosphere.

It didn't. In fact, neither she nor Zack said much throughout the meal, both of them allowing Mandy to babble on about Sugar. As she related everything Zack had told her about the mare's history to Lesley, one thing came through quite clearly: Zack must have spent a small fortune on the animal. The Appie was one of the top horses on the rodeo circuit and, at eight years old, still had a few years of competition left in her.

Why he would think Mandy needed such an expensive piece of horse-flesh, Lesley couldn't imagine, but she was too tired to worry about it now. Her day had started at four-thirty a.m.—her shift at the coffee-shop started at six—and what with the ups and downs since she'd got home, compounded by two glasses of wine with the meal, she could barely keep her eyes open.

She was concentrating on doing just that when Mandy suddenly fell silent. When she looked over to her, her daughter yawned broadly and stretched. 'I'm sorry. Mom, is it OK if I go to bed now?' She got out of her chair and started around the table to kiss her mother goodnight.

Lesley just stared at her. Granted, her daughter had been up almost as long as she had, and had had a full day as well. However, her daughter had greater energy reserves then Saudi Arabia, and had never in her life volunteered to go to bed without prompting.

'Don't you want to stay up until your dad leaves?' Lesley asked.

Mandy glanced over to her father and a look passed between them. Lesley frowned slightly, then her daughter was saying, 'He understands I'm tired. Goodnight, Mom.' She planted a kiss on Lesley's cheek, dropped one on her father's and was gone.

Lesley's frown deepened as she looked after her, then her gaze drifted idly to the flickering candle-flame. Oh, no. She almost groaned. Mandy was matchmaking again—tactfully leaving her and Zack alone. Zack was probably in on it too, if that look that had passed between them was anything to go by.

It wasn't going to do them any good, though.

Gathering together the plates sitting in front of her, Lesley said briskly, 'I expect you'd like to be moving on yourself. It's a long drive back to Cheyenne, and it'll be long past midnight by the time you get there as it is.'

She started to rise, but Zack's hand came out and caught her arm, holding her in her chair. 'Actually, I wanted to talk to you about that.'

The touch of his hand on her arm was doing nothing for her composure and she pulled free of his hold. With her hand safely on her lap, she eyed him cautiously. 'What's there to talk about it?'

Zack leaned back in his chair and rubbed the side of his face with his palm. He seemed to be searching for words, and Lesley felt a flutter of dismay. She had a feeling she wasn't going to like those words when he found them.

Finally, he leaned forward again and rested his elbows on the table. 'I was wondering if I could stick around here for a few days.'

Lesley started shaking her head, even before he finished the sentence. No, no, no.

'Come on, Lesley, I haven't seen Mandy since Christmas. I know it was my fault that I couldn't have her at Easter, but give me a break. All I want is to have a few days with her. You get to have her around all the time, but I don't get that chance.'

Guilt reared its ugly head. Hadn't she vowed earlier that she wasn't going to be possessive of Mandy? It wasn't fair to either Zack or Mandy, but having him here . . . She just couldn't. That earlier kiss was too fresh in her mind. He could still arouse her. It was purely a physical thing, probably triggered because he had been her first and only lover. But, for whatever reason, she knew she'd be a fool to ignore the danger of having him staying in the same house with her.

'So, what do you say?' he prompted.

'Why don't you take her back to Cheyenne with you?' Lesley suggested. 'It wouldn't hurt for her to miss a few days of school.'

'I doubt if she'd want to leave Sugar just when she's got here. Besides, I think it would be a good idea for me to keep an eye on her until she's completely used to the new horse.'

Lesley shot him a look of dislike and he met it with a faint smile. He always had an answer for everything. When they were married, quarrelling with him had been an exercise in frustration. His arguments had come off as well thought-out and logical, while hers had seemed over-emotional and unreasonable.

Well, maybe she was an over-emotional and unreasonable person—because she didn't want him staying here! She was going to tell him so, too. Her blue eyes taking on the light of battle, she met his gaze.

Before she could speak though, he forestalled her. 'I know it would be a little awkward, but I really would appreciate it if you'd give it a try. I'd keep out of your way. I've got the camper and wouldn't even have to stay in the house. Just let me park it in the yard. I really do want some time with Mandy.'

At least he wasn't asking for her to provide him with a bed. Lesley studied him, a tiny, puzzled frown creasing her forehead. Unless he'd changed radically over the years, he wasn't acting in character. It wasn't like him to . . . well, almost beg for something. It would have been more in keeping if he had just told her he was staying and she could like it or not.

'Is spending time with Mandy the only reason you want to stay?'

She saw his faint start, but when he answered his tone was bland. 'What other reason could there be?'

That was just it . . . what other reason? Then suddenly she knew. Wasn't he the same man who shortly after Mandy's birth had gone out and spent several hundred dollars on an imported English baby carriage when she'd been at her wits' end trying to figure out how they would pay the hospital bill?

She gave him a wry look, sighing faintly. 'You don't change, do you, Zack? Why don't you just admit it?'

His own look was shuttered and somehow wary. 'Admit what?' he asked slowly.

'You're broke, aren't you? That's why you're so keen to stay here—you haven't got any place else to go. It's just so typical of you—spend your last dime on a stupid gesture like buying that horse, and end up needing a place to bunk down.'

'That's what you think? That I'm penniless?' In the dim candlelight, Lesley missed the anger that had steeled his dark eyes, and interpreted the harshness of his voice as embarrassment.

'Well, don't worry about it,' she dismissed airily. Standing up, she scooped up a stack of dishes. 'Now that I know the reason, I won't turn you away. You can stay as long as you like—but in your camper!' With that parting shot, she disappeared through the door to the kitchen.

Stern-faced, Zack shoved his chair back, ready to follow her and set the record straight, then stopped himself. The ire evoked by her insulting accusation faded, and amusement started to take its place. It was really kind of funny when he thought about it. Here he'd been, afraid she might be trying to cash in on his success with Sheridan Inc., but she apparently didn't even know about the company. In fact, she thought he was destitute.

And, if he wanted to stay around for a while, he wondered if maybe he shouldn't let her go on thinking that.

He got to his feet, gave the remaining dishes a guilty glance, and left the room. He should help Lesley clean up—she looked tired—but he had to talk to Mandy before her mother did. He hoped she hadn't fallen asleep yet.

She hadn't. As soon as he opened the door to her bedroom, the bedcovers were thrown back and Mandy scrambled into a kneeling position.

'Is she going to let you stay?' she asked.

He nodded, walking over to switch on the bedside-lamp before going back to shut the door quietly. Seating himself on the edge of the bed, he said. 'She said I could stay as long as I wanted.'

'Oh, super! We're going to have so much fun.' The bed rocked as she flung herself into his arms. Zack hugged her briefly, then tucked her back under the blankets.

When she'd calmed down a little, he said, 'I wanted to ask you something. You haven't mentioned anything about my stores to your mom, have you?' Sheridan Inc. was a chain of equestrian outlets located throughout the west. He'd first invested in it five years ago, the first year he'd been top money winner on the professional rodeo circuit. Two years ago, when he'd retired from rodeoing, he'd bought out the other shareholders. Since then, he'd been investing his heart and soul into the company. They sold every accoutrement a horse-man could possibly want, from hoof picks to horse-trailers.

He'd taken Mandy into the Cheyenne outlet several times when she'd been staying with him, and had made no secret of the fact that he was the owner. He was surprised she'd never told Lesley—in a way, he'd wanted her to. He was proud of his success as a businessman, and had wanted his ex-wife to know he wasn't the irresponsible rodeo bum her parents had always accused him of being.

But Mandy obviously hadn't said anything. He looked at her now, noting the colour mantling her curved cheeks and the way she avoided his eyes. 'I'm not upset with you, honey. I just thought it was odd you never mentioned it to her.'

'I wanted to,' Mandy admitted, keeping her eyes lowered to the bedspread she was fingering nervously. 'It's just . . . well, Mom's kind of funny. She . . . she likes you.' She looked up suddenly, her dark eyes so like his own, earnestly seeking his. 'I know she likes you,' she repeated. 'Only—well, every time I started to tell her about you, she sort of changed the subject or found something she had to do right then, so . . . I just kind of quit saying anything.'

'I see,' Zack said heavily. Despite Mandy's reassurance that Lesley 'liked' him—obviously designed to spare his feelings—it was pretty obvious her mother wanted nothing to do with him.

'I'll tell her about your stores tomorrow,' Mandy offered when he remained silent for several moments. 'I'm sure she'll think it's really neat.'

'Oh, no. That's just what I don't want you to do.'

If he'd had any doubt, he was convinced now that Lesley's soft-heartedness was the only reason she had agreed to let him stay. It rather placed him in the category of a homeless dog. It wasn't an idea he particularly relished, but for Mandy's sake he guessed he would have to put up with it for a while.

He gave her a tender glance. She was so young, so vulnerable. He wasn't going to let her childhood be ruined by letting her mother marry someone she couldn't abide. He'd been around Mandy's age when his widowed mother had remarried. He hadn't like James Brooks from the beginning, growing to hate him as the years passed. When he was fourteen, he'd finally run away from home. Lying about his age, he'd got a job on a ranch up near the Montana-Wyoming border. The owner, Jeremiah Turner, had turned out to be a good friend, almost a father to him. His son, Jerry, had been like a brother, and the rancher had taught the two of them calf-roping and rodeoing.

But, even though things had turned out well in the end, the price had been hard. Though the Turners had been almost family to him, they couldn't make up for the hurt he'd suffered from his stepfather. He hadn't been able to forgive his mother either, and had remained estranged from her right up until her death a few years ago. He didn't want that kind of life for his daughter.

'Why don't we just keep Sheridan's our little secret?' he asked of her. 'It's a little joke I want to play on your mom.'

Mandy was obviously puzzled, probably wondering what kind of sense of humour her father had, but finally nodded.

'Good girl.' He stood up and reached down to

rearrange the blankets, before dropping a kiss on Mandy's forehead. 'It's time you were asleep, young lady, so get those eyes closed,' he ordered with mock severity.

Giggling, the child scrunched her eyelids tightly shut and he grinned down at her. 'Goodnight,' he whispered, snapping out the light and leaving the room.

Lesley was at the sink, washing dishes, when Zack returned to the kitchen. She wasn't aware of his presence at first, and for a moment he stood in the doorway looking around the room. He'd visited the farm frequently in those first days after Lesley had come back here with the baby, and this room didn't seem to have changed at all. Even the calendar hanging over the chrome and formica kitchen-table might have been the same except for the date. The same herd of baleful-looking Herefords still looked out at him.

It should have been a cheerful place, with its bright homey wallpaper and gingham curtains at the windows, but the eerie sensation of *déjà vu* that was creeping over him made him uncomfortable. Any minute he expected the outside door to open and Roy Hammond to walk in. His worn, sun-burnt face would be set in a scowl, and there would be no welcome in those hard blue eyes.

Lesley's mom hadn't been like that, but in some ways she'd made him feel worse. A thin, nervous woman, she'd sent him skittering, fearful glances, afraid he was going to take her ewe lamb with him when he left.

But damn it all, Lesley had been his wife—she should have gone with him. He looked over to her now and a wave of emotion he couldn't control swept over him. He wanted to walk over to her, slip his arms around that slim waist and bind her to him. He wanted to feel that warm, responsive body in his arms again. He wanted her beneath him, clinging to him and crying his name as he pulled her with him to heights of passion.

Unexpectedly, she turned from the sink and caught him watching her. 'Oh!' she said, startled. 'I thought you'd gone out to the camper already.'

He drew a deep breath before answering her but, none the less, his voice was harsh. 'I went up to check on Mandy.'

He mentally berated himself. He must be going crazy to have let his thoughts drift into those channels. Lesley wasn't even his type any more. In the years since the divorce, he'd developed a connoisseur's taste in women. He liked them full-busted and leggy, decked out in designer clothes and smelling of exclusive perfume. The kind of woman he went for wouldn't have been caught dead in the cheap cotton skirt and blouse Lesley was wearing, her pale blonde hair dragged back in a ponytail with untidy wisps hanging about her face. His features hardened. His ex-wife was too thin, her pale face shadowed by fatigue and devoid of make-up. He liked a woman of leisure, someone who spent her time making herself beautiful for him. Not someone up to her elbows in dishwater.

Lesley gave him a puzzled look, seeing the grimness in his expression; 'She wasn't still awake, was she? We have to get up pretty early, and she's going to be cranky all day if doesn't get enough sleep.'

'She was awake, but I told her to get to sleep.'

'That's good,' Lesley replied awkwardly. She

turned back to the sink and resumed washing the dishes. If he'd told her in that tone of voice, the poor kid would probably have nightmares. What was the matter with him?

He stared at her back, the slight droop of her shoulders. She was carrying this downtrodden scullery maid business a bit far. 'You look like hell,' he said suddenly. 'Why don't you leave those until the morning and go get some sleep?'

For a moment, she was too startled by the abruptness of his attack to react, and stared dumbfoundedly down at the bubbles in the sink. Then her temper flared and she swung around to face him.

'Well, I'm sorry I don't meet with your approval,' she sneered. 'I usually do get to bed earlier than this, but unfortunately, I had a guest for dinner. I can't leave the clean-up until tomorrow because I have to be at work at six. There won't be any time to do them before I leave.'

He glared back at her, his mouth curling cynically. 'Do I hear violins in the background?' he asked. His eyes flicked away from hers then riveted back on to her blue ones. 'You always did love playing the martyr, Lesley. Is this little act all for my benefit? I'm flattered.'

'What do you mean by that crack?' she demanded.

He pointed to the side of her. ' "A woman's work is never done." There's a dishwasher right beside you. All you've got to do is load the dishes into it and turn it on. Even I'm domesticated enough to figure that out.'

Lesley sputtered at him, too angry for words, especially when he yawned and said, 'Well, you'll have to forgive me if I walk out in the middle of your performance, but I think I'll get some shut-eye.'

He turned on his heel and walked away. The saturated dishcloth she threw at him thudded against the outside door and slithered to the floor as he slammed it behind him.

CHAPTER THREE

WHEN the radio alarm sounded the next morning, Lesley only just restrained the impulse to switch it off and bury her head back under the covers again. The sun hadn't yet risen, although the sky was streaked with crimson dawn and the birds that roosted in the cotton-woods surrounding the house had started their morning concert. In her body, it still *felt* like the middle of the night. However, she couldn't afford to sleep in any longer. She had a hard enough time getting through her morning chores before setting off to work, without the delay of dawdling in bed.

She struggled out of the bed and dragged on jeans and a sweatshirt. She always did the outside chores first, letting She-Ra out of the kennel where the collie had spent the night, and feeding Toby . . .

She hesitated as she zipped up the jeans. There'd be Sugar and Clancy waiting for oats this morning as well. She hadn't remembered in those sleep-drugged minutes before getting out of bed. Zack was here.

No wonder she was so tired this morning. Not only had she got to bed late, but she'd lain awake for a long time afterwards, wondering how was she going to cope with having him here. When she'd been washing dishes last night, before he'd joined her in the kitchen, she'd convinced herself she'd made the right decision in letting him stay. She *had* been

37

married to him. It seemed almost her duty to help
him out when he was down on his luck. Besides,
wouldn't it be good for Mandy to have her father
with her on her own territory, at least for a few days?

That quarrel, though . . . Mandy wasn't going to
benefit from watching the two people she loved most
in the world tearing strips off each other the minute
they got together. That kind of dissension had been
one of the reasons she'd divorced him. Granted, it
had usually been Zack and her dad going at each
other whenever Zack had come to see her; however,
they'd argued too. Mandy had been very upset by
the bickering, couldn't understand the atmosphere
of tension that hovered over the house whenever her
father had come to see them. In the end, the only
solution had seemed to be to cut him out of their
lives. Zack wouldn't give up the rodeos, even though
by that time he'd made enough money for them to
settle somewhere, and Lesley wouldn't go back to
him, as long as he stayed on the circuit.

But he was back in their lives, in *her* life again. He
had probably told Mandy he was staying when he'd
gone in to check on her last night; he'd said she'd
been awake. She was stuck with him now, and she
had an awful feeling that she was going to regret
having him around all the time.

At least she wouldn't be seeing him this morning.
Zack never had liked getting up early. Lesley bit her
lower lip as she started down the stairs for the
kitchen, firmly turning her mind from that thought.
It would be only too easy to remember how they'd
spent those early-morning hours when Zack had
wanted to linger in bed.

When she pushed open the kitchen door, the rich
aroma of freshly brewed coffee poured forth. The

overhead light was on as well, and Lesley blinked against its harsh glare as she stepped into the room. Zack was standing at the stove and turned to smile at her.

'Good morning.'

'Good morning,' Lesley returned his greeting cautiously. Now, what was going through that handsome head of his? He'd been like a bear with a sore head last night when he'd walked out, and now he was handing her a cup of coffee as pretty as you please and looking as if butter wouldn't melt in his mouth.

She took a sip of the brew, then set the cup down on the table when she realised she didn't have time to drink it now, anyway.

'I have to feed the horses and let She-Ra out. I'll drink this later.'

'Don't rush off. Sit down and I'll fix you some breakfast,' Zack said placidly. 'I already turned the dog loose, and I'll take care of the horses later.'

Lesley stood staring at him. She knew what was going on. She *had* turned off the alarm this morning and gone back to sleep. This wasn't even happening. It was all a dream!

Her dream ex-husband seemed awfully real, though, when he came over to her and, after taking her arm, pulled out a chair from the table and set her in it. 'Just sit here and enjoy your coffee while I cook you some bacon and eggs. You look like you haven't quite woken up yet,' he teased, leaving her to go to the fridge and get out the breakfast supplies.

'You can say that again,' Lesley muttered.

'What did you say?' Zack asked, when she thought he hadn't heard her.

'Nothing.'

He shrugged, moving to the stove and starting to arrange strips of bacon in the skillet he had ready. 'You still like your eggs over-easy?' he asked over his shoulder.

Obviously this wasn't a dream, and she didn't think it was much of a joke, either. 'What's going on, Zack?' she demanded aggressively, getting to her feet. 'You went out of here last night in a dirty temper, and now you seem to think you're Betty Crocker. What's all this in aid of? Hell, you don't even know how to cook!'

'I was coping alone even before you divorced me, so don't be so surprised that I learned my way around a stove,' he retorted, revealing that the mood of last night had not totally disappeared.

She matched his gaze defiantly, but her mouth quivered and her hands were trembling. Damn, why did he have to come back into her life, upsetting its even tenor?

'I'm sorry,' he relented, subduing his temper. 'I know I was a bit of a beast last night, and I wanted to make it up to you. Won't you sit down and let me fix you something to eat? Look at it as sort of a peace offering.' He smiled coaxingly at her, and she hesitated, finally nodding. Mandy would be up soon, and she didn't want her child walking in on a scene.

Silently, she resumed her seat and moodily drank her coffee. After a few minutes, Zack brought over two heaped plates of bacon and eggs and set them on the table. As she watched him limp back towards the stove to get the coffee-pot, she snapped, 'Oh, sit down and rest, I'll bring the coffee over.'

She stood as he turned back to her. 'I'm not helpless, Lesley,' he said coldly.

The hard anger in his eyes forced her back into her chair. 'Sorry,' she muttered. She wasn't at her brightest first thing in the morning. She shouldn't have said anything, but she would have been uncomfortable having him wait on her even if he hadn't been lame.

She didn't look at him as he brought the coffee-pot over and refilled her cup, returning the pot to the stove before taking his own place at the table. After a few minutes, the silence grew strained. Nibbling on a slice of crisp bacon, Lesley surreptitiously slid him a glance. He looked remote and unfriendly. However, she guessed she was to blame: he'd started out friendly enough. From the set of his jaw, though, it looked like it was going to be up to her to make the overtures now. 'This tastes good. I usually just have cold cereal.'

For a moment, he didn't say anything, but continued eating. Finally, he must have decided he'd make an effort as well and said, 'I suppose you don't have time for much else. You must be pretty busy around here in the mornings.' He looked up from his plate, catching her eye. 'I expect you're pretty busy most of the time. I'm sorry I gave you a hard time about looking tired last night. You probably had every reason to be.'

Though she didn't like being pitied any more than he did, at least he was trying to get along with her. Doing her part, she smiled and said lightly, 'I'm busy, yes, but it's not that bad. I got a little carried away with supper last night. I don't usually cook anything so elaborate on the days that I work.'

'Why don't you find an easier job?' he suggested. 'There must be something else you could do, work in an office or even a dress shop.' Lesley murmured something non-committal and he continued, 'Why have a job at all? I'd think just looking after Mandy would be enough.'

A hard edge had crept into his voice, and Lesley shot him a resentful glance. She worked hard at making sure Mandy wasn't neglected. Oh, she admitted she would love nothing better than to make caring for her daughter her only job. She was a homebody at heart and had never had any desire to be a career woman. However, the pair of them had to eat and her job took care of that. Besides, there were a lot worse ones in this world.

'This is the best job I've had since I started working. It's a little grim having to be at work so early, but it means I'm off early in the afternoon and I'm *always* home for Mandy when she gets back from school.'

He didn't seemed impressed, but went back to eating his breakfast without comment.

She gave him a sour look, then caught a glimpse of the wall clock. Seeing the time, she stuffed the last bite of her toast into her mouth, and swallowed hastily. 'I'd better get moving. It's already after five, and Mandy isn't even up yet. I drop her off to stay with the Sheppards in the mornings until the school bus comes.' While Lesley was talking, she was moving, taking her used dish to the sink and turning on the tap.

Zack followed her, putting his hands on her shoulders to move her away from the sink. 'You go get Mandy up. As long as I'm staying, let me pitch in and do my share. I'll do the dishes.'

She was justifiably surprised, since he obviously didn't approve of her working. On the other hand, she was loath to look a gift-horse in the mouth, especially when she was running late. However, when she noticed his eyes slide to the dishwasher, she knew she had to say something. 'You have to do them by hand because the dishwasher's broken.'

She waited for him to withdraw his offer, but he merely said. 'OK.' He did give the machine a considering look, though. 'When's the repair man coming?'

Lesley frowned, then realised she'd have to be honest. If Zack stayed around for any length of time, he'd soon find how things stood. 'He isn't,' she said flatly. 'It's been broken for months. I haven't had the money to get it fixed.'

She swung around and walked towards the door. 'Look, I've got to get Mandy moving.' She knew he wanted her to go on talking, give him a chance to ask questions, and for once she was glad mornings were so hectic.

Lesley was letting Mandy have a slumber party for her birthday that night, so she left work early to prepare for it. Not having to stay for her full shift all the time was one of the perks of her job, and she hadn't lied when she'd told Zack it was the best one she'd ever found. Perhaps if she hadn't had Mandy she would have looked for one that paid more money and had a little more challenge, but, as a working mother, she found that her waitress job had a lot going for it. The manager of the coffee-shop was very understanding and didn't mind if she clocked out early once in a while, or didn't come in at all if Mandy was ill and home from school.

And, as today was Friday, she had the whole weekend ahead of her to spend with her daughter. She always had weekends and holidays off as there were plenty of highschool girls willing to work those hours. In June, one of those same girls would relieve her for the duration of the summer school vacation, so that she could spend it with Mandy. It wasn't a paid holiday, so that meant there wasn't any money coming in until September when she went back to work, but with careful budgeting they managed. Lesley felt the lost wages were insignificant compared to the advantages of being a full-time mother again for a few months.

It wasn't until she reached home and saw Zack's rig still parked over by the barn that she remembered she had forgotten to tell him about Mandy's party. He might change his mind about staying around here when a hoard of giggling little girls descended on him, she thought humorously.

When she went into the house, she found him standing in the middle of the kitchen. Something was different about the room and she hesitated, trying to pin it down. It was noise, a low hum combined with the splash of water. It was coming from the dishwasher!

She stared at it, then turned her gaze to meet Zack's broad grin. 'You fixed it?'

'Sure did,' he confirmed. His voice was rich with pride, and she felt its echo in her own heart. Zack had always been good with his hands. The old pick-up they'd run when they were first married had always been breaking down, yet somehow her husband had always got it going again. Although they joked about its running on prayer and curses, it was Zack's talent that kept it out of the junk yard.

She'd been proud of her husband's skill. As they continued to smile at one another, Lesley realised she was experiencing the same pride in him she had in those days. Self-consciously, she looked away. He was no longer her husband. She no longer had the right to feel proud of his accomplishments.

Zack's voice broke what was threatening to become an awkward silence. 'I found a piece of bone in the rotor impeller. That's why it wasn't pumping the water out,' he explained, which didn't exactly enlighten Lesley. 'While I had it apart, I replaced some worn wires and hoses. I found the stuff out in the shed where your dad's tools are. I hope you don't mind my snooping around in there.'

Lesley shook her head. 'I don't mind at all. I think. It's just super you got it running again. Thank you, I've really missed it.'

It really had been thoughtful of him to get it running again, though she wasn't quite sure how to express her gratitude. Aware of his eyes on her, she walked over to the machine and gave it a loving pat. It was that or throw herself into Zack's arms, and she didn't think the latter would be wise. Tempting, but not wise.

It was still tempting when he moved to join her in front of the machine. 'I thought I'd better run it through all its cycles empty before we loaded it. I might have only screwed things up.'

'Oh, I'm sure you didn't.' She kept her head lowered because she could feel heat creeping up her cheeks. At his nearness, she could feel the warmth radiating from his lean, tough body; smell the clean, male scent of him. She'd dated other men since their divorce, but they could have been robots for all the sexual interest they'd aroused in her. Only with Zack had she ever felt this magnetic pull of primitive chemistry. It wasn't fair, either. She wanted to treat him like an old friend, not have to constantly battle against this physical awareness she had for him.

He reached past her to pick up the screwdriver he'd left on the counter, and his arm brushed her shoulder. It sent a shockwave of sensuality shooting through her that caused her to jump.

Zack looked at her curiously and, when she kept her head down, slipped his hand beneath her chin to raise her face to his. She closed her eyes briefly, then knew she had to try to meet his. As soon as she did, she saw by the change of his expression that he could read her thoughts. They'd been married, she'd borne his child. He knew her body and her responses as well she knew them herself.

He set the tool back on the counter as his arm slipped around her back. 'Lesley?' he questioned softly.

At his touch, she knew she was lost. She moistened her lips in invitation, and he didn't wait long to accept it. His warm, firm lips covered hers as his hand dropped from her chin to caress her full, waiting breast through the thin nylon of her uniform dress. As he drew her against him, she succumbed to the spell of his embrace, moulding her form to his and drowning in the sensual ecstasy of his kiss.

For a timeless moment, they kissed. With his tongue and lips he explored the welcoming softness of her mouth, firing her blood and sending her pulse-beat soaring. He eased his hand from between them and moved it to her hips. He lifted his head and whispered, 'What does time Mandy get home from school?'

Dazed, Lesley stared up into his desire-lit eyes, her own luminous with passion. 'Why?' she asked stupidly.

His mouth twitched into a smile, and he brushed

her temple with a light kiss. 'Guess why I want to know?' With his hands on her buttocks, he tightened his hold. She could feel his hard arousal pressing against her abdomen, and swallowed with difficulty. When it had started she hadn't thought of where their kiss might lead—she'd only thought of the sweet pleasure of being in his arms again.

'Oh, dear,' she muttered. The smile on his face faded to a faint frown. When she placed her hands on his shoulders to disengage herself from his embrace, he let her go.

Putting a few feet between them, she faced him. 'No, Zack, I don't think so.'

He appeared calm and unruffled, but she couldn't tell what he was thinking. 'Why not?' he asked presently. 'We're two consenting adults. Hell, we've even been married, so we wouldn't be doing anything we haven't done many times before. What's wrong with having a little afternoon recreation?'

That was just it. That's all it would be to him: an enjoyable interlude, nothing more, nothing less. It would be sex, pure and simple. It was totally illogical for her to want it to be anything more, but . . . how could she forget that, when they had been married, they'd made *love*?

Her eyes skittered to his as he waited for her to say something, then quickly shied away. She'd started it and probably did owe it to him to explain why she was calling a halt now. Unfortunately, she couldn't think of any explanation that wouldn't make her sound like a prudish idiot. All she came up with was a lame, 'I don't think we should.'

'Not even for old times' sake?'

'Not even for old times' sake,' Lesley repeated

firmly. In the tense silence that followed she wished she smoked—it would give her something to do with her hands and then maybe she wouldn't feel so damned awkward. Finally she said, 'I'd better get busy. I'm baking Mandy a birthday cake this afternoon.' She made a move towards the fridge to get out the milk and eggs.

Zack stared at her, then suddenly threw his head back with a shout of laughter. Bewildered, Lesley stopped where she was and watched him. When he sobered, she still hadn't figured out what it was he had found so funny, but at least he wasn't angry, so she offered him a tentative smile.

'You're priceless,' he said. 'I'm not in any danger of becoming a bighead while I'm around you, am I?'

'I don't know what you're talking about,' Lesley admitted, still not understanding the joke.

Grinning, he turned around and gathered up the screwdriver and other tools he'd left lying on the counter. On his way out of the kitchen, he stopped in front of her and smiled down into her puzzled countenance. 'I've never considered myself a super-stud, but I do have a certain amount of conceit. After what we had together, I never thought the day would come when you'd pick baking a cake over an hour in bed with me.' Planting a quick, hard kiss on her parted lips, he walked out of the kitchen.

'This isn't going to work.' Unwittingly, Lesley said the words aloud, startling herself in the quiet kitchen so that her hand jerked as she was manipulating the icing bag and she botched her 'Happy Birthday'. She had a quick look around to make sure Zack hadn't come in without her noticing, then found a knife to scrap off the misshapen 'B' and redo the letter.

Whether she said it aloud or to herself, though, it was still true. It was *not* going to work having Zack around all the time. It would be just too much of a strain. She knew a lot of divorced women ended up having affairs with their ex-husbands. Virginal brides, faithful wives, as divorcees they just didn't feel comfortable about becoming intimate with someone else. It wasn't surprising they turned to their old lovers for fulfilment of their sexual needs.

However, even if her sex-life had been nothing to write home about for the past five years, she didn't want to start sleeping with Zack again. If staying celibate was going to start getting her down, she'd find another solution. She'd been seeing Brian Collins for months and felt sure that he would oblige if she decided to move her relationship with him on to that plane. She was very fond of him, and maybe it was about time she started thinking of him as a lover instead of a friend. As soon as he got back from his business trip to Arizona, she was going to seriously consider it. It would make a lot more sense than falling into Zack's bed again, even if what they had had together—at least, in that department—had been pretty special.

Unfortunately, her mind was still on that thought when Mandy came skipping into the kitchen a moment later. She'd been so preoccupied by it that she hadn't even heard the school bus. Although she knew quite well her daughter couldn't read her thoughts—and hopefully wouldn't understand them if she could—she still blushed furiously.

'Anything wrong, Mom?' Mandy asked, stealing a glop of icing from the bowl as she studied her mother's burning cheeks.

'I've had the oven on all afternoon, so it's warm in here,' Lesley improvised hastily. Wanting to divert her attention, she stepped back from the counter and gestured to the cake. In addition to the salutation and a few rosebuds, she outlined a fairly creditable horse's head in chocolate icing in one corner. 'What do you think? It looks pretty good, if I do say so myself.'

'You did a great job! Thanks, Mom.' Mandy gave her a quick hug and asked. 'Now that it's done, can we go and hire the videos for tonight?'

Lesley smiled wryly—so much for the hour she'd spent decorating the cake. Already, Mandy was moving on to other considerations and—damn, she'd forgotten her promise to take her into town to pick a VCR and a couple of films for her party. It was going to be a bit of a mad rush to do that and finish the preparations for the party before the guests descended on them. However, she had promised . . .

'I can run her in,' Zack offered from the doorway while Lesley was still dithering. She hadn't heard him come in.

'Oh, can Daddy take me?' Mandy begged, before Lesley could collect herself enough to respond. 'I haven't had a ride in his new pick-up yet.'

'Well . . . er—I don't mind if your father doesn't.' Her daughter's enthusiasm wasn't exactly flattering. She looked over to Zack. 'You can get them over at the grocery store in Platteville.'

'We won't be gone long, then.' He held his hand out for Mandy and she moved to join him, but Lesley delayed her.

'Just a minute.' Her purse was on the kitchen table, and she went over to it and got out some money. Taking it over to give to Mandy, she asked,

'And what kind of movies can you get?'

'I know, rated PG,' Mandy said sulkily, then brightened. 'Can I get a horror movie?'

Lesley made a face. 'I don't want a bunch of little girls up all night with nightmares.'

'We're not babies,' her daughter protested.

Not wanting to get into that kind of discussion at this point, Lesley reminded her that her father was waiting for her. It served the purpose, and Mandy shot out the door past him. Zack held back for a second and, when Lesley glanced at him, said, 'I could have paid for the movies. It'll only be a few dollars and I'm not quite that broke.'

'I didn't say you were,' Lesley said placatingly. He still looked offended, though, and she was suddenly annoyed. If he hadn't been here, she would have gone with Mandy, helped her choose what she wanted to see. The least Zack could do would be to let her pay for them. 'Look, Zack, you got her the horse. Isn't that enough? I know you've always accused me of being tight-fisted . . . too worried about tomorrow and what bills it would bring to enjoy life, but I love Mandy. I might not be able to make extravagant gestures like you do without counting the cost, but I do like to give the occasional treat . . . ones that I can *afford*.'

'I see.' Stony-faced, he turned to follow his daughter. Maybe it had been a cheap shot, but right this minute she just didn't care.

CHAPTER FOUR

WITH Mandy's guests cocooned in their sleeping-bags on the floor, the living-room looked as if it was suffering from an infestation of giant caterpillars. The light from the television flickered ghoulishly across their engrossed countenances as Lesley picked her way through them.

Gaining the door, she slipped through it into the welcoming brightness of the kitchen, firmly closing it behind her and shutting out an eerie crescendo of organ music.

On shaking legs she walked to the cupboard and took out a cup to pour herself a coffee from the pot keeping warm at the back of the stove. She almost dropped it when the door behind her opened. As she swung around, her eyes were wide with terror until she saw it was only Zack. In her relief, semi-hysterical laughter bubbled up in her throat and she swallowed it hastily.

'You OK?' he asked.

She took a deep breath and swallowed again before saying, 'Of course. I just came out for some coffee. I'm fine.' The trembling hand she raised to push back a strand of hair that had fallen across her pale cheek belied the statement.

'You don't look fine,' Zack remarked as he walked over to her. He reached up and ran his fingers down her pallid cheek. Her milky-white skin was clammy to the touch, and a slight frown knitted his forehead. 'You should have stayed in here when the movie started. You know horror movies upset you.'

Lesley lowered her eyes and shrugged. The faint pink of embarrassment was bringing colour back into her cheeks. She should have known he would guess what was wrong: they'd been married, lived together, and he knew her foibles. 'I feel such an idiot,' she admitted shakily. 'I don't even believe in any of that stuff . . . vampires and demonic possessions. It's just . . .' She trailed off, gesturing with her hands helplessly.

His expression was indulgent, his brown eyes tender as they rested on her downbent head. 'It's not your fault. You have a lot of imagination, and I suppose those movies react on you like a closed room does on someone with claustrophobia.'

Having him make excuses for her only made her feel that much sillier. She was a grown woman, after all. It was ridiculous the way she fell to pieces watching a simple film.

'I don't know what those kids must think of me,' she muttered. 'They're lapping it up and I'm hiding in here, scared out of my wits.'

As she still didn't look up at him, Zack patted her shoulder in a comforting movement, then left his hand resting on it. 'Come on, I doubt if they even noticed you left the room. Don't worry about them. Besides, this is all my fault, anyway.'

'Your fault?' She lifted her head to look at him then.

'I should have paid more attention to what movies Mandy was getting. When we got to the store, I saw John Murray in the car park. I haven't seen him in years, so I stayed outside and chatted with him while Mandy went in to pick out her films. Before we left home, she seemed to know which ones she was allowed to have, so I didn't check up on her when I went in to sign for them and carry out the machine.' His face took on a stern expression that didn't bode well for his daughter. 'Obviously, I shouldn't have trusted her.'

'Oh, don't be too hard on her,' Lesley said philosophically. She stepped slightly closer to him in a conciliatory motion, and it seemed natural for his arms to slip around her waist in a loose embrace. 'You know how kids are, give them an inch . . . I didn't actually *say* she couldn't rent a horror movie, and since it's her birthday she probably figured she could get away with it.'

'Well, I don't know that she should,' he replied grimly. 'You looked pretty upset when I followed you in here.'

'Well . . . yes.' She shuddered involuntarily as the image on the screen that had sent her scurrying in here flashed through her mind. Zack pulled her closer to him and, seeking comfort, Lesley rested her cheek against the hard wall of his chest. It wasn't a sexual embrace, but one of comfort that brought warmth seeping into the very marrow of her bones. His arms were firm and secure around her, creating a haven from the irrational fears brought on by her fertile imagination. His heart beat reassuringly against her ear and slowly the remaining vestiges of tension within her uncoiled.

'Mom!'

Their daughter's eruption into the kitchen shattered the moment of closeness. Lesley jumped back from Zack, pulling free of his arms and swivelling to look at the child.

For a moment, Mandy's face was a study of bewilderment, but then a brilliant smile slowly dawned over her childish features. Her dark eyes brimmed with joy and hope as they moved between her parents.

Appalled, Lesley stared wordlessly back at her. How was she ever going to explain? It had been a moment's weakness, a space out of time . . . not the reconciliation her daughter so obviously thought it was.

'Mom, Dad?' Expectation threaded through her daughter's voice like a silver strand.

Lesley glanced over to her ex-husband, seeking his support. He was smiling at Mandy with calm affection, nothing in his manner suggesting that he was experiencing any of the turmoil that she felt. He was completely ignoring his daughter's obvious misinterpretation of the scene she'd walked in on.

Maybe that was the best response, Lesley thought. Explanations would only draw more attention to something that was essentially nothing—meaningless. Sliding Zack another glance and taking in his composure, she knew it *had* been meaningless.

'Did you need something, sweetheart?' he asked his daughter matter-of-factly.

'I—er . . .' Mandy stammered. Confusion was edging out the glowing expectation in her eyes. Lesley turned away from her and moved to pick up the coffee-pot from the stove.

'I was just about to go back in and watch the end of the movie,' Zack said smoothly, walking over to the child. 'Tell me what you want and I'll get it for you.'

Lesley didn't turn back around to face them, but

continued to stand by the counter sipping her coffee and trying to regain her equanimity. 'The movie's over,' she heard Mandy telling her father. 'We were going to start the other one, but Tina says she wants to go home now.'

'Go home? I thought your friends were all staying for the night.'

'They are, but Tina says she doesn't feel too good, and wants to go home.'

Zack looked down at her sternly. 'This wouldn't have anything to do with the movie you picked out, would it? She's probably just scared. Your mother told you not to get a horror movie.'

'That's not what she said,' Mandy defended herself cheekily, then looked instantly apprehensive when she caught her father's expression. Hastily, she switched back to the original subject. 'Tina says she feels sick and wants to go home.'

Zack didn't answser immediately, and Lesley set her cup down suddenly, seizing on the opportunity for escape. Turning to face the others, she said, 'I'll go have a look at her. She's probably just homesick.' Skirting a path around the other two, she fled to the living-room. She was pretty sure Zack was going to give Mandy a dressing-down for disobeying her over the choice of movies. Lesley had been planning to ignore the transgression, even though she knew she shouldn't let Mandy get away with disobeying her. She felt guilty about relinquishing the unpleasant task of disciplining her to Zack, but left it to him none the less.

Pulsating rock music broke over her in waves as Lesley waded through the sea of giggling pyjama-clad bodies in the living-room, looking for Tina. She spotted her sitting quietly in one corner. Lesley frowned slightly. The other girls were taking advantage of the intermission to do a little experimenting with make-up—with results more theatrical than seductive—but her mother's instinct told Lesley that the flush mantling Tina's cheeks was due to temperature and not rouge.

'Aren't you feeling well, honey?' Lesley asked when she reached her. Kneeling beside the girl, she slipped an arm around her.

Tina hunched her shoulders in misery. 'I'm sorry, I just want to go home and see my mom.'

She sniffled, and Lesley knew tears weren't far off. She ran an experienced hand over the child's forehead and felt its heat. 'You feel kind of warm,' she acknowledged. 'Would you like me to drive you home?'

Tina nodded desolately and muttered, 'Please.'

She doubted that there was anything seriously wrong with Tina; it could just be over-excitement or, as Zack had said, she was scared. Whatever it was, looking down at the child's woebegone face, Lesley knew she'd have to take her home. Children wanted their own mother when they were under the weather, and someone else's just wouldn't do.

'OK, that's what I'll do,' she said bracingly. 'You'll be home with your mom in just a few minutes.' As she stood up, drawing the girl with her, she heard the phone ring. 'I'll go see who that is while you get your things together. You don't need to get dressed, just wear your dressing-gown home OK?'

The girl gave her a watery smile and nodded. 'Thank you, Mrs Mackenzie. I'm sorry I'm so much trouble.'

'It's no trouble. I'm sure your mom would do

the same for Mandy.'

The phone had stopped ringing by the time she started threading her way back towards the kitchen. Zack must have answered it, because Mandy had already rejoined her party. As she passed her, Lesley saw her daughter heavy-handedly applying crimson red lipstick to her rose bud mouth, looking very pleased with herself. Her father couldn't have been too hard on her, although some of her exuberance had dimmed. Lesley gave the chaotic room a surveying glance. She hoped he wasn't going to let Mandy off that easy if she and her friends got any of the junk they were putting on their face on to the carpeting. The moment the thought entered her head, Lesley immediately wondered why she assumed *Zack* would be the one to deal their daughter.

The telephone was situated on the wall by the kitchen table, and the receiver was lying on the table-top when Lesley came into the room. Zack was seated on a chair beside it and gestured to it. 'For you.'

'Thanks for answering it,' she said stiffly, aware that her ex-husband's look was strangely intent as she lifted the mouthpiece and spoke into it. 'Hello?'

'Hi, it's me.' She recognised Brian's voice immediately.

'Brian! Good of you to call. Are you back in Denver, or are you still in Arizona?'

'Arizona, unfortunately. By the way, who answered the phone?'

Lesley's eyes slid to Zack. He seemed to have taken a permanent lease on that chair. She sent him a speaking look, but, instead of getting up and going into the other room, he leaned forward and rested his elbows on the table. Resting his chin on his hands, his mouth curved into a Cheshire-cat smile.

Pointedly, she turned her back to him. 'That was just Zack, Mandy's father.'

'Your ex-husband? I didn't think he came around much. What's he doing there?' Brian's voice expressed surprise and curiosity, but no jealousy—at least, none that Lesley could detect over the phone line.

Lesley opened her mouth, but she couldn't get the words out. Eavesdropping on every word she said, Zack *deserved* to hear her tell Brian he was stony broke and was staying here because he didn't have anywhere else to go. She couldn't though, and she was afraid that the reason had little to do with not wanting Brian to know that Zack was actually staying here for some time. Finally she said, 'He got Mandy a new horse for her birthday and brought it over for her.'

'So how is she enjoying her birthday?' Brian asked, easily diverted on to the new topic. That was one of the things she liked about him. Another man might worry the subject of her ex-husband's unexpected presence to death, but Brian hadn't a jealous bone in his body.

'She's having a great time. She's having a slumber party tonight and the living-room looks like a bomb hit it. Would you like me to go get her so you can talk to her? She hasn't thanked you for the ghetto blaster you gave her . . . forgive me if *I* don't.'

His laughter reached her clearly through the phone line. 'Wishing I hadn't given it to her?'

'Well, let's just say "blaster" is the operative word,' Lesley retorted drily. 'I guess my eardrums will survive though, and she's really delighted with it. Let me go fetch her and she can tell you herself.'

'Don't bother. I'm sure she doesn't want to be dragged away from her company,' Brian said good-naturedly. 'I really just called to let you know it'll be a few more weeks before I can come home. This project we're working on is running into quite a few snags.'

'Oh, Brian, I was really looking forward to you coming back.' Until she heard the wail of dismay in her voice, she hadn't even known herself how much she was looking forward to Brian's imminent return. While she wanted to see him for his own sake, more importantly, he would have provided her with a buffer against Zack.

'Well, I'm sorry, Lesley,' he apologised, 'but I'm afraid I don't have much choice. The company wants to get this land deal put together as soon as possible so they can start construction.' Brian worked for a big property development firm based in Denver. It was a responsible position: finding and purchasing sites for their projects, dealing with all the zoning changes and permits needed to get them underway. He was currently putting together a shopping centre project in Phoenix, and Lesley knew he couldn't simply abandon it because she wanted to use him as a defence.

'Well, I'm really going to miss you,' Lesley said unhappily.

'I'll see you as soon as I get back,' he assured her. 'We'll take Mandy on a picnic up into the mountains. How would you like that?' He sounded disconcerted, and Lesley supposed he had a right to be. Although they dated regularly when he was in Colorado, it was a relationship based on companionship and mutual interests. Part of her attraction for him, she knew, was that Mandy and herself offered him a taste of family life, without his having to give up his bachelor existence. Although they kissed, in most ways theirs was a brother-sister style relationship. It was little wonder that he was surprised to hear Lesley go on like a pining mistress about his delayed return.

'That sounds great. I'll let you go now. I have to drive one of Mandy's friends home because she isn't feeling well,' Lesley said, deciding it might be best to end the conversation. She was beginning to feel a little awkward. She'd been fairly confident of Brian's co-operation if she decided to become his mistress in reality. However, she was now beginning to wonder if it would be that easy.

She was mulling this over when she turned back to Zack after hanging up the phone. The Cheshire-cat pose had vanished, taking the smile with it. Now he reminded her of another kind of cat, one that was infinitely more dangerous: a panther waiting to spring. As he regarded her from beneath half-closed lids, she felt a tingle of apprehension run along her spine.

'So that was the famous Brian,' he stated.

She nodded, then distractedly rubbed her temple with her fingertips. This was really weird. They'd been divorced for five years, and yet Zack looked and sounded almost jealous. And, as for herself, she felt almost as guilty about the thoughts that had been going through her mind as if she had still been married to him and contemplating infidelity. This just wouldn't do.

Her head lifting haughtily, she met his dark eyes with challenge in her own blue ones. 'Yes, that was Brian.'

'I heard you ask him if he wanted to talk to Mandy.'

Lesley wasn't quite sure where he intended taking this conversation, so she answered cautiously. 'That's right. He said not to bother taking her away from her friends.' His brows quirked sceptically and her lips thinned in anger. She didn't know exactly what he meant by that mocking gesture, but she was sure about one thing—she didn't like it.

However, the sounds of laughter and music coming from the other room reminded her that this wasn't the time or place to start rowing with him.

'I told Tina I'd drive her home,' she informed him coldly. 'I'll go see if she's ready.'

As she started for the door, Zack got to his feet. His tall, lanky form blocked her path and she halted. 'I'll take her,' he offered.

She watched him limp to the door, but before he went through it he hesitated and turned around. In some indefinable way, his expression had changed and he somehow looked friendlier now. Lesley relaxed slightly: she hadn't really wanted to quarrel with him. She smiled enquiringly at him and he smiled back at her. 'I was just wondering, are you sleeping with that guy?'

She'd been prepared for him to ask her where Tina lived, and so was caught totally off guard by the question. 'No!' she blurted out, then, 'It's none of your business whether I'm sleeping with Brian or not.'

He grinned at her. 'I was just curious.' Without another word, he went through the door, whistling tunelessly.

*   *   *

After giving the cleared table a final wipe with her cleaning cloth, Lesley lifted the grey rectangular tub she'd set the used dishes in and started towards the kitchen. The Columbine Café where she worked was located off the foyer of the Prairie Inn motel. It was a pleasant establishment, with maple tables and captain's chairs scattered over the gaily patterned carpeting, and lace-trimmed calico curtains over the windows. With a reputation for serving good food at reasonable prices, the restaurant was a busy, popular eatery among local residents as well as travellers. However, at this time of the morning the dining-room was nearly empty. The lull gave Lesley and the other waitress, Estelle, an opportunity to recover from the breakfast rush.

As Lesley approached the other woman seated at the end of the lunch counter, she saw her quickly stub out her cigarette and jump to her feet. After a quick glance in the direction of the doorway, Estelle turned to Lesley and said, 'I'm finished. You can have your coffee break now.'

Lesley stared at her, her look puzzled. 'But you've hardly sat . . .' She saw Zack approaching them and didn't finished the sentence. It didn't really matter, as Estelle wasn't listening to her anyway. The other woman's attention was firmly focused on Lesley's ex-husband.

'Good morning,' she called to him while Lesley eyed him with dismay. What was he doing, following her here? She'd managed to avoid him quite successfully for most of the weekend. Saturday she'd spent setting the house to rights after Mandy's party. As she'd been engaged in a frenzy of mopping and scouring, he'd fled with their daughter on a long horseback ride—it was that or risk being sucked up in the vacuum cleaner. Sunday, she'd taken herself off to the shopping mall in Greeley, leaving before the other two were up and not retuning until nearly supper time. Any time that she hadn't been able to avoid being in his presence, Mandy had been with them and had proved to be a very efficient buffer.

'Good morning,' Zack returned Estelle's greeting, but walked past her to join Lesley. 'My timing's pretty good. Since it's time for your break, you can keep me company over a cup of coffee.'

'I . . .'

'You two know each other?' the other waitress demanded. She gave Lesley a hostile look. Although she was almost forty, Estelle none the less fancied herself the reigning *femme fatale* of the coffee-shop, and expected first crack at every presentable male that walked in—and Zack was certainly that. Although casually dressed in a plaid western shirt and jeans, he exuded an aura of maleness that would have commanded the attention of even the most discriminating of females.

And Estelle was hardly that—discriminating, that was. Estelle was *very* female. Her critics claimed she would latch on to anything in trousers. Whether it was true or not, Lesley was one of the few waitresses who could work with her in harmony, and that could have been because she quite happily left the field to her co-worker. Oh, Lesley enjoyed a mild flirtation as much as the next woman, but had soon learned that the indulgence had its pitfalls. It passed the time when things were slow, but when you were trying to juggle orders for a dozen tables, and some fellow came in expecting you to drop everything so that you could drool all over him, it was nothing but a nuisance.

'I'm Zack Mackenzie, Lesley's husband,' he introduced himself to the other woman.

'Her husband?' Estelle exclaimed, eyeing Lesley with avid curiosity. Come to think of it, Estelle had a lot of faults. Aside from being a man-eater, she also loved gossip. 'Shame on you, Lesley! You never told me you had this lovely man tucked away.'

'Zack is my *ex*-husband,' Lesley grated out between clenched teeth.

Zack slipped his arm around the small of her back. His fingers dug into her midriff and she was forced against his side. He smiled down into her furious eyes. 'We're still good friends though, aren't we, darling?'

She would have kicked him if weren't for the fact that Estelle was already going to make enough out of this encounter to keep her the main subject on the motel grapevine for the next week. From the amused glint in Zack's eyes, she could tell he knew exactly what thoughts were going through her head. It made her want to kick him all the more.

He turned his attention back to the other waitress. 'How about getting us a couple of cups of coffee, honey, while we go sit down?' Without waiting for an answer, he moved towards one of the booths over by the window. As his arm was still around her waist, Lesley had perforce to go with him.

'If you insist on having coffee with me, at least you could have let me get it,' Lesley hissed. 'Estelle isn't going to be too pleased about having to wait on me.'

They had reached the booth, and Zack released her to let her slide on to one of the benches, then took his seat across from her. 'I wanted to talk to you without the company of our little pitcher and her big ears, so I thought I'd catch you at work. Having gone to all that trouble, I wouldn't want you running off to hide in the bowels of the kitchen.'

Lesley pressed her lips together. That was exactly what she had planned to do, but he'd caught her all right. She thought she knew just what those calves he roped felt like.

CHAPTER FIVE

THEY sat in silence until a disgruntled Estelle brought them over two cups of coffee. Even after she'd left, Zack didn't open the conversation. Lesley added cream and sugar to her coffee, and sampled the brew. With the silence lengthening, she finally asked testily. 'So, what did you want to talk about?'

He stirred his coffee diligently, a delaying tactic since he drank it black. Finally, he looked up and answered her. 'I guess I want to know what you're doing working here.'

'I wish you would get off my back about my job,' Lesley complained. 'What's wrong with this place?' She gestured around her. The Columbine Café, wasn't exactly the main dining-room of a luxury hotel, but it wasn't a dive either.

'Well, if you like it so much, how come you're taking the summer off?' Zack retorted. At the look she gave him, he added, 'Mandy told me.'

She would have loved to have shouted at him to mind his own business, but Estelle was standing over by the counter watching them. Lesley didn't think she could overhear their conversation, but she would if things were to get heated.

'I always like to take the summer off so I can spend it with Mandy. Satisfied?'

'No,' he said flatly. 'I don't see why you're going out to work at all.'

'I suppose it never occured to you that I might

67

need the money,' Lesley came back acidly.

'Oh, it occurred to me,' Zack said grimly, '*after* you told me you couldn't afford to get your dishwasher fixed. But before that . . .' He looked across to her, his eyes taking on a softer light as his expression coaxed. He reached out and covered the hand she'd left resting on the table with his own. 'What's happened, Lesley?' he asked gently. 'Your dad must have left you more than just the farm when he died. He used to go on for hours about how successful he was at farming, what a good provider he was.'

As she heard the note of bitterness in her ex-husband's voice, Lesley bit her inner lip in contrition. Roy Hammond had never let up on his son-in-law during all the years of their marriage. *He* could give his daughter and grandchild lasting security, something an irresponsible cowboy could never do. Oh, maybe Zack would have a few good years rodeoing, but what would happen to them when he got too old or too crippled to follow the circuit any longer?

'Was he lying about all that?' Zack interrupted her thoughts.

Lesley looked away from him, shaking her head. If she had hung on to her anger, she might have been able to come up with a snappy retort and avoid answering him.

At last, she cleared her throat, though when she spoke her voice was still husky with emotion. 'It wasn't really a lie. Not that he was John Paul Getty or anything, but he did leave a reasonable estate. It . . . things were a pretty big mess at that time. You know he and Mom were in a car accident?' Zack nodded, the pressure of his hand covering hers encouraging her to continue. 'Well, he was killed right away, but Mom . . . she lived about three months. There was a lot of brain damage so she didn't suffer, she never even regained consciousness.'

'Go on,' he prompted, even though he was aware of the pain in her voice.

Lesley pulled her hand free and, resting her elbow on the table, cupped her forehead in her palm. She addressed her cooling cup of coffee. 'I don't know what you know about hospitals, but—well, they're pretty expensive. Mom was in intensive care the whole time. Dad's insurance didn't even begin to cover the cost. He'd saved quite a bit of money over the years, but faced with those kind of bills, it didn't last long. When it was gone, I sold off all his farm equipment. The neighbours were really great. They knew the kind of fix I was in, but also knew I couldn't just accept money outright. They organised an auction and everybody bid everybody else up. I got a lot more for it than a dealer would ever have given me.'

She sighed, then forced herself to go on. 'Anyway, that kept things going for another few weeks, and when it ran out I took out a mortgage on the farm. Mom died just before I'd spent it all.'

She dropped her hand and looked over at him, her eyes shimmering with tears. 'I felt so damned guilty about it when she went. I was so relieved that I wouldn't lose the farm along with everything else. I know it wasn't as though she was even alive—her brain was irrevocably damaged and she'd have never known me or Mandy again. But she was my mother and when she was dead all I could think of was that the bills would finally stop. It was as if the money was more important than she was, and in some weird way I'd wished her death.' She put her hand to her mouth and clamped the side of her finger in her teeth to try to stem the tears that were threatening to spill over. Even after four years, that awful nagging guilt still overwhelmed her whenever she remembered her mother's passing.

'Don't feel like that, Lesley,' Zack said softly. 'You're only human, and naturally you felt relieved. Your father worked incredibly hard all his life to build up what he had. In this day and age, the individual, independent farmer trying to make a living off the family farm has a tough time just surviving. For your dad to have achieved the financial success that he did is quite remarkable. You had every reason not to want to see it all expended on a hopeless cause, especially when doctors' car parks are filled with Cadillacs and Mercedes, and hospitals have become big businesses, as concerned with profit margins as they are with saving lives.'

She found comfort from his words, especially knowing how difficult they must have been for him. It took a big man to acknowledge the worth of someone who'd always treated him with disdain. She shot him a look of gratitude.

'You're wrong about the doctors' car park: Mom's doctor drove a Ferrari,' she said sardonically. However, she was feeling a little better. 'I'm sorry about dumping all that on you. Let's talk about something else.'

He hesitated, then said, 'Before we do, can I ask you something? Didn't you ever think of getting in touch with me at that time? I mean, you must know I would have helped you out.'

Lesley licked her lips, clasping her hands in her lap and studying them intently. She'd thought about it, of course. The temptation to run to Zack during that awful three months had been overwhelming at times. But . . . she just couldn't.

'We were divorced, Zack,' she said quietly.

'I know, but that doesn't mean you couldn't have come to me for help.' There was a colouring of hurt in his tones, and Lesley felt a dart of guilt. The divorce *had* made a difference, though. For one thing, she wasn't even sure now if she'd have ever filed for one if her parents hadn't been behind her, pushing her into it. It hadn't seemed right somehow to run to him when her problems were so centred around them.

She knew he was waiting for her answer, and finally she shrugged. 'It was a long time ago, and what with the way things were between you and my folks . . . It doesn't really matter now. I managed.'

'But since then you could have let me know how things were with you. I've never given you a nickel of alimony or child support. You have a right to expect that from me. If I'd had any idea of how things stood, I would have gladly paid. It just never occurred to me that you might need financial help. You should have told me. You sure as hell didn't need to go out and get a job as a waitress,' he said heatedly.

'I've told you, my job isn't that bad,' Lesley placated, aware that his voice had risen and Estelle might hear them. She leaned forward towards him. 'Look, Zack, can't you just quit worrying about it? In some ways, it was better for me to have things the way they were. After my parents died, I was forced to learn to stand on my own two feet. As awful as it was during those months when Mom was in the hospital, at least the experience made me grow up. As long as I lived with Mom and Dad, I didn't have to—they took care of me just like when I was a little girl. After they were gone, though, I found I had to accept adult responsibilities. It wasn't so bad, either.'

'I never treated you like a child. If you'd have lived with me as my wife when they were still alive, as I wanted you to do, you would have grown up a lot sooner.'

'Maybe I would have,' she admitted, then hesitated. He wasn't going to like the next part, but she forced herself to go on. 'On the other hand, it might not have made any difference. Neither one of us were very responsible when I was going with you on the circuit. I mean, we never worried about the future, building for it. Whenever you won anything at the rodeo, we'd go out and blow the lot on steak dinners and new clothes and saddles and God knows what else. It didn't seem to matter that between wins we lived on macaroni and cheese because we couldn't afford anything else. It was fine when there was just the two of us, but after Mandy was born, somebody had to provide her with security. My parents did that for her as well as for me.'

'And you didn't think I could have ever done that?' he asked angrily.

'Could you have?' Lesley returned wearily. 'I know you were making good money just before you quit, but what about since then? What if I *had* got used to depending on an alimony cheque from you every month? Where would I be now? As much as you disparage my job, at least I know I can count on it to keep groceries on the table. Right now, you can't even take care of yourself, let alone me and Mandy.'

She picked up her coffee-cup, preparing to leave him. Given the looks Estelle had been shooting at her for the past few minutes, it was a wonder she could still go back to work and wasn't dead on the spot. However, as Lesley's fifteen-minute coffee break had lasted three-quarters of an hour, her co-worker had every right to be annoyed.

Before she could slide out of the booth, though, Zack caught her by the wrist and delayed her. 'What if I wasn't broke? What if I told you that I had invested the money I earned on the circuit and now I'm perfectly capable of providing for you and Mandy? What would you say to that?'

She glanced down to her wrist, gently twisting it to disengage it from his hand. He left her go and she got to her feet. Zack would never change, and in a way she was glad he hadn't—that she hadn't been able to force him to. His impulsive 'live for today and let tomorrow take care of itself' nature had been one of his attractions in the first place. It wasn't until after Mandy had been born and she was back living with her parents that she'd realised she couldn't live her life as he did. Day after day, her father and mother had drilled into her the need for security, for a solid foundation on which to build a life for Mandy and herself.

Their warnings had frightened her, kept her clinging to their nest. Zack would one day leave her a penniless widow, they'd predicted. They'd been nearly right, Lesley thought as she studied her husband's face. Here they were years later—Zack was broke and, although thankfully he hadn't been killed, he had been permanently lamed by a bull.

Knowing that she had been right to heed her parents' warnings didn't give her much satisfaction though. Zack was just the way he was, and it didn't feel right to hear him pretending to be something else.

Her smile was a little sad as she looked down at him. She had hurt him with her home truths, and she was sorry about that. However, he had to know she couldn't take him seriously.

'I guess I'd say that my job isn't as secure as I thought it was, because any minute I expect the drug squad to bust in here and close us down for serving you whatever was in that coffee.' She reached down and picked up his empty cup, then leaned towards him, her voice dropping to a conspiratorial undertone. 'Just to be on the safe side, I'll go destroy the evidence.'

That evening, after supper, Lesley wandered rather desolately through the house. Zack had driven Mandy to her horse club meeting and, although she had expected him to just drop her off and come back, as the time passed she knew he must have decided to stay.

The problem was that there wasn't much to do around the house. Her cleaning blitz on Saturday had caught up on all the housework and the place looked almost as good as when her mother was alive. Her mother had been very houseproud and had liked nice things around her. The furniture was all of good quality and, although Lesley hadn't replaced anything since her death four years ago, it was still a comfortable and attractive home when it was clean.

Finally, Lesley settled in the living-room to read one of the books she'd got from the library in

Platteville that afternoon. She'd gone after work, mainly because she hadn't wanted to get home before Mandy and be forced to spend time alone with Zack. That being the case, it was rather silly for her to be feeling lonely and sorry for herself because he'd decided not to come back to the farm while Mandy was at her meeting.

She wasn't very successful in her reading, and had only reached page ten of the book when she heard Zack's pick-up returning a couple of hours later. She probably couldn't have told anyone what was in those ten pages, either. However, she tried to present the picture of an engrossed bookworm when Mandy, followed by her father, came into the living-room a few mintues later.

She closed the book with feigned reluctance and looked at her daughter. 'So, did you have fun at your meeting?'

'It was great,' Mandy assured her, coming to sit on the arm of the sofa next to her. She draped her arm across her mother's shoulders. 'Everybody's going to come over here on Saturday. I want to show them how fast I can run the barrels on Sugar.'

Lesley gave her daughter a chastening scowl. The horse would deserve most of the credit. In a regular competition, the speed with which the horse and rider could run a clover-leaf pattern around three barrels set in an arena depended on the competence of both the animal and the rider. However, Mandy wasn't that proficient a rider at this point. An exhibition on Saturday would be purely a display of the horse's training and ability.

'Your dad didn't get you that horse just so you could show off on her to your friends,' Lesley reminded her.

'I know that,' Mandy grudged, looking faintly guilty. That was exactly what she'd wanted to do. 'They're not coming here just so they can see Sugar. Daddy said he'd give us a demonstration of roping. We'll just practise on the barrels afterwards.'

Lesley glanced over to her ex-husband who was still standing by the door, wondering whose idea this had been. It meant that Zack would have to stay until the weekend at least. Had he been planning to stay that long, or was Mandy cajoling him into it?

Zack walked further into the room and took a seat in the chair opposite her. 'I didn't say that exactly. Mandy and her friends cooked up this scheme, and I said I'd go along with it, if you had no objections.'

'But you don't mind, do you, Mom? Everybody can come over, can't they?' Mandy got in before Lesley could speak.

'I guess I don't mind,' Lesley replied. She looked at Zack. 'Are you sure it's OK with you? I mean, it isn't going to interfere with your plans, is it?'

'I'm looking forward to it,' Zack assured her.

'That's fine, then,' Lesley said meekly, quelling her frustration. He had completely ignored her hint to expand on just what his plans were, and she was reluctant to ask him in front of Mandy. When she'd offered to let him park his camper-truck in the yard, she hadn't thought too much about how long he might be staying, though she had assumed it wouldn't be longer than a few days. Zack was a born gyspy, always on the move.

It seemed he was going to be here until Saturday at least, and, as she watched her daughter skip over to him and snuggle into the chair beside him, a little worried frown creased her forehead. The longer he stayed, the harder it was going to be for Mandy to see him go—and he would go eventually.

'Don't you think you should be getting ready for bed? It's past your bedtime,' Lesley interrupted her daughter as she appeared bent on turning the rest of the evening into a long planning session of Saturday's activities.

Mandy pulled a face. 'Everybody else in my class at school gets to stay up until ten.'

'Aren't you lucky to be unique, then?' Lesley replied placidly, then her voice hardened. 'Now, go get ready for bed.'

Mandy cast a hopeful look up at her father's face. His reply was to plant a brief kiss on her childish mouth, then shove her out of the chair and on to her feet. 'Do as your mother tells you. Goodnight.'

Looking put out, Mandy shuffled over to Lesley and touched her lips to her mother's cheek in a reluctant salute. She was half-way to the door when she turned around. 'Could I have a snack before bed?'

Lesley shot her an impatient look. It was Zack who answered, though. 'There were refreshments at the meeting. You've had enough to eat tonight, so quit making excuses and go straight to bed.'

'All right,' Mandy sighed in a hard-done-by voice. On leaden feet she dragged herself from the room, and a few moments later they heard the door to her bedroom upstairs slam. Zack and Lesley exchanged a look of dry amusement.

'It's tough being a kid,' Zack remarked, standing up. 'I guess I'd better be moving on as well.'

'You're going?' she asked, the note of dismay in her voice causing Zack to hesitate. Now that Mandy was out of the way, she had planned to lead him around to telling her how long he was planning to stay. She hadn't been expecting him to leave immediately, although now that she noticed it, he hadn't removed his windbreaker when he'd come in. Zack was watching her and she scrambled to her feet, knocking her book to the floor. She bent over to retrieve it, then straightened.

'I thought . . . would you like to stay for a few minutes and have a drink with me? There's some wine left from the other night, or I've got some beer.' She'd put on her dressing-gown and slippers before settling down with her book earlier, and now she self-consciously tightened the belt of the robe. It was made of a heavy terry cloth and not the least seductive; she could feel her face flushing under Zack's speculative gaze. She wasn't planning a tête-à-tête, just a friendly discussion on what he intended doing over the next couple of weeks.

After several moments, Zack finally nodded. 'That would be nice. I wouldn't mind a beer.'

'I'll get you one then. Coors, OK?'

'Sure.' She saw him start to unzip his jacket so he could remove it, and fled to the kitchen to get the drinks.

CHAPTER SIX

WHEN she returned to the living-room a few
moments later with the beer for Zack and a small
glass of wine for herself, she hesitated in the
doorway. Zack hadn't returned to the chair he had
originally been sitting on, but was lounging on the
sofa next to where she had been sitting. He looked
casual and very much at home. A secret smile of
amusement tugged at her lips. However Zack had
interpreted her invitation, he didn't appear to expect
a simple question about his travel plans!

As she walked towards him with the drinks, his
eyes did a lazy survey of her form and her amusement fled. Somehow the thick dressing-gown didn't
seem quite as all-enveloping as it had before, and
she felt a frisson of tension shimmer over her
skin.

She hastily thrust the beer into his outstretched
hand, and a tingle of shock raced up her arm as their
fingers brushed. Startled, she met his eyes, then
couldn't look away.

'Thanks.' His eyes never left hers as he took a sip
from the glass. Zack had sexy eyes, bedroom eyes,
deep, seductive brown eyes fringed by long black
lashes. He could seduce a woman with those eyes,
she thought shakily. She hastily jerked her gaze
away from his.

'You're welcome,' she acknowledged huskily,
backing quickly into the chair across from him.

Trying to ignore the speculative look he gave her at her choice of seat, she took a quick swallow of her wine, then looked to him with studied equanimity. His pale yellow cotton shirt was unbuttoned at the neck, exposing the dark, curling hairs of his chest. The denim of his jeans stretched taut across his thighs as he leaned back. He'd been raw-boned and gangly when she'd married him, but then he'd only been twenty. At thirty-two, his shoulders had filled out, his chest broadened. It suited him. He'd always been attractive, but now . . .

She resisted the urge to jump up and turn on the overhead lamp. She hadn't noticed how dimly lit and atmospheric the living-room appeared with just the table-lamps on.

The silence stretched uncomfortably as she waited for him to say something, but he seemed content to simply watch her while taking an occasional sip from his beer.

'I read in the paper today that there's not much snow in the mountains this year. I guess that means we'll all be short of irrigation water this summer.'

'I suppose so,' he agreed indifferently.

As that line of conversation obviously wasn't leading anywhere, Lesley cast around for another one. The weather . . .? She caught a glimpse of mockery in his eyes. He knew she was ill at ease, and suddenly decided that she'd had enough of small talk.

'I was wondering how long you were planning on staying here?' she asked baldly.

His eyes narrowed slightly, and he shifted to sit more upright. 'Anxious to see the back of me?' he asked.

Lesley stared down at the wineglass clasped in her

hands. She swirled the pale gold liquid briefly, then took a sip. She'd be lying if she said she was anxious for him to go. Even after a few days, days she'd made an effort to avoid being around him, his presence had none the less been felt. Like Mandy, she was going to find it a hard adjustment when he wasn't here any more. However, there was no doubt in her mind that he *would* leave sooner or later.

She looked up to find him watching her. He'd leaned forward, his elbows resting on his knees, the beer glass cradled in his hands. 'I just thought you'd probably want to be moving on soon, maybe go look for a job.'

'Actually, I have a job.'

'You do?' The surprise in her voice was hardly flattering, and she saw his mouth twist bitterly. 'I mean . . . I thought . . .'

'Yes, I know what you thought,' he responded sardonically, and Lesley flushed. He took a long swallow from his glass, draining it, and set it aside. 'You've heard of Sheridan's?'

'The equestrian supply outfit? You work for them?' She gave him a disconcerted look. No matter how hard she tried, she couldn't imagine Zack working in a store, serving customers . . . directing ladies to the fitting-rooms to try on jeans!

'I'm not a sales assistant,' he read her thoughts.

'Oh, I see.' He must work in the warehouse. She glanced at his leg, frowning slightly. There would be a lot of lifting and running around in that kind of job.

'What does this Brian fellow do?' he asked abruptly.

'Brian?' Lesley echoed, startled by the aggressiveness suddenly evidenced in his tone.

'Yes, this Brian that you go around with. What does he do for a living?'

Remembering the last time he'd questioned her about Brian, she grew cautious. However, she answered him mildly enough. 'He works for a property development firm in Denver. He's sort of their advance man, setting up projects, buying property, that kind of thing.'

'Sounds impressive. He must be an important man in the company.'

If Zack worked in a warehouse, she supposed it did sound that way to him. Lesley lowered her eyes, shrugging matter-of-factly. 'I suppose so,' she downplayed.

'And he must make good money,' Zack probed further.

'Yes, I guess he does.' She looked up and caught the look of contempt that marred his handsome features. It took a moment for it to register, but when it did her temper sky-rocketed. 'Just what are you suggesting, Zack? That I go out with Brian because I'm some kind of cheap little gold-digger after his money?'

'Well, are you?' he retorted, unscathed by her fury. 'Money seemed to be the crux of our problems when we were married. I can't see you taking on another poor man.'

'Money had nothing to do with why I divorced you,' Lesley cried heatedly.

'Didn't it?' he jeered.

Lesley jumped to her feet, her eyes blazing. 'No, it didn't!' At his sneer of disbelief, she lost all restraint, shouting, 'Tell me, what happened to your leg? Some bull did that to you, didn't it? I knew that it would happen some day, that or you'd be killed.

Well, I couldn't take waiting for it to happen any more.'

He seemed stunned by her impassioned outburst, staring mutely back at her, his face losing colour. She swung her back to him, covering her eyes with her hands. Her breath came in shuddering gasps, her pulse thundering in her ears. She felt Zack come up behind her and put his arm around her shoulder.

'I'm sorry I said those things, Lesley. I didn't mean them, and I know they weren't true,' he said contritely. 'Come on now, don't cry.'

'I'm not crying,' she said wearily, dropping her hands from her pale face. She was disconcerted to see that they were trembling. For a moment, in the aftermath of that fierce anger, she had wanted to cry, but not any longer. Now, she only felt deadly tired.

Zack was looking down at her in concern and she managed a weak smile. 'I'm sorry I shouted at you. It just made me mad that you seemed to think I could be so mercenary. I thought you know me better than that.'

'Lesley . . .'

'Mom, what's going on? I thought I heard shouting.' Mandy was standing in the doorway, her dark hair rumpled and her eyes heavy with sleep.

Lesley moved abruptly away from Zack and his arm dropped to his side. She stared helplessly at her daughter, not knowing what to say.

Zack recovered more quickly. 'It must have been the television. We just turned it off.' He walked over to the child. 'I'm sorry we woke you up. Say goodnight to your mom again and I'll take you back up to bed.'

Mandy looked worriedly from Zack to her mother, then yawned and rubbed her eyes. 'I'm sleepy,' she informed them unnecessarily.

'Then you'd better get back into bed,' Lesley said, striving to inject a light tone in her voice. 'Goodnight, honey.'

'Goodnight, Mom,' she said as Zack lifted her into his arms and bore her away.

When he came back into the room alone a few minutes later, Lesley walked to the living-room door and closed it carefully. She turned to face him, leaning back against the door. Her face was pale and very determined.

'I think you should leave, Zack.'

He eyed her from his stance in the centre of the room. 'Mandy's gone back to sleep already. I think we should finish our talk.'

'Our talk is finished. Our marriage was finished five years again. There's nothing left between us now but cold ashes. We're accomplishing nothing by stirring them up.' She held his eyes resolutely, even as she watched them slowly freeze over. 'And when I asked you to leave, I didn't mean just this room. I want you to leave the farm, get in your pick-up and go back to Cheyenne. It's just not working having you here.'

'And what about Mandy? What'll you tell her?'

'She must know that you'll be leaving sooner or later. This is just sooner, and she'll get over it. It's better than you staying and having her listen to us quarrel. You can stay until the morning so that she can say goodbye. I'll say goodbye right now.' Lesley moved from the door and walked towards the sofa where Zack had left his windbreaker. Her limps felt heavy and cold, just like her heart, but he had to go. She picked up his jacket and held it out to him. 'Goodbye, Zack.'

Zack didn't move. 'No, Lesley,' he said quietly, but his words were weighted with determination. 'I'm not leaving.'

'I've asked you to leave, Zack. I don't want to fight about it.' He didn't reply, and finally she was forced to lower the arm holding his windbreaker as it started to tremble. Her nerves was stretched near the breaking point, but she knew she couldn't give in to him.

'I don't want you here,' she reiterated. 'I agreed to have you here because I thought you needed a place to stay. You obviously don't. You said you had a job—go back to it, go back to Cheyenne and just leave me alone. I don't want you.'

'Oh, yes, you do,' Zack stated deliberately, the hard set of his features sending a wave of trepidation washing over her. 'Maybe there is nothing left of our marriage but ashes, but you still go up in flames whenever I touch you. I want you, I want you back in my bed.'

'No, Zack.' Lesley resisted, backing away from him until her knees came up against the sofa and forced her to stop. 'No, I'm not going back to you. You know it wouldn't work, we tried marriage once . . . for God's sake, let's not make the same mistake twice.'

'I never said anything about getting married again.' He smiled derisively, slowly advancing towards her. She forced herself to hold her ground, even though her mouth was dry with fear. This was a Zack she had never seen before, there was a ruthlessness in him that she hadn't known existed.

'I won't have an affair with you, Zack.' He

stopped in front of her, with mere inches separating them. She trained her eyes on the third button of his shirt, daring to looking no higher.

'Won't you, Lesley?' he asked with soft deliberation. He stroked a finger down the curve of her neck, then rubbed it along the V-neck of her robe. She shivered under his touch, fighting against the desire to melt against him. He was right, he was so right. His touch did set her aflame, but she couldn't let it consume her.

He continued in a low, seductive pitch, 'I was your first lover, as you were mine. We taught each other what it was all about. There's never been anyone since who was quite the same.'

Jealousy, like hot, burning acid, seared through her brain. She'd never been jealous of him when they'd been married, and the emotion caught her off guard. 'There have been others?' She couldn't stop the words from spilling out.

His chuckle reproved her. 'You didn't think I took a vow of celibacy just because you dumped me, did you? Naturally there have been others.'

His mockery triggered anger and gave her the impetus to jerk away from him. However, he captured her easily, restraining her with his hands around her waist. Her blue eyes blazing with rage, she glared up at him. 'Let me go. Go back to one of them and leave me alone.'

'You sound jealous, dear wife. No need to be, I told you, you were special.' His head started downwards, his lips seeking hers.

'I'm not jealous, just repulsed,' she gasped, twisting her head and shoulders to evade him. The movement caused them to overbalance and they fell to the sofa together. Zack held himself over her, taking his weight on his elbows, but his legs firmly pinned hers. Lesley's face was pale as she looked up into his, pale not just with anger, but with fear—fear of herself, fear of her traitorous need.

He smiled down at her, the turn of his mouth smug. 'Isn't this cosy?' He lowered his head to gently brush her brow with his lips. They trailed over her temple until they reached the shell of her ear. With his tongue, he explored the delicate shape of it, then gently nibbled her lobe. 'Mmm,' he murmured. 'Remember that night your folks went to that Grange meeting and we stayed here? We made love for hours on this same sofa.'

How unfair of him to remind her! She remembered, and despaired as the sweet memory undermined her opposition. 'Please let me up,' Lesley choked.

'I'm not hurting you, am I?' He shifted slightly to ease his weight from her. With his change of position, though, she became aware of the hard swell of his manhood pressing against her thigh. Words dried in her throat. She knew if she said 'yes' he'd leave her, and that was what she should do. However, she could only stare mutely up into his face.

Her determination to stand fast against him was being consumed by the sensations he aroused within her. His touch, his body over hers, set her alight, kindling a flame of passion that burned primitive and hot. His hand had insinuated itself beneath her robe and was working its way up her midriff towards her breast. He reached his goal and, as his palm closed over her throbbing breast covered only by the thin material of her nightie she involuntarily arched towards him.

Until that moment there had been a sense of almost clinical detachment in his movements, but at her response a tremor ran through him. 'Oh, God, Lesley, I want you,' he groaned, burying his lips in her throat. With ardent hands he tore aside the heavy terry of her robe, then pulled the neckline of her nightgown downwards. As his mouth closed over her swollen nipple, she shuddered, all reticence lost in the flood of primal hunger flowing through her.

When he lifted his head and raised his body away from her, she clutched at him with desperate hands. He smiled down at her, gently removing her hands, and swung his legs off her to sit beside her. 'Sit up,' he ordered, his arm going behind her back to help her.

Bemused, Lesley complied. He slipped the loosened robe from her shoulders. 'Let's get some of this out of the way.' Their eyes met and held. He lifted her hands to his chest, cradling then against his heart. 'Feel how it beats for you. Undress me.'

His hands dropped away from hers, and Lesley's fingers fumbled with the buttons of his shirt. They lingered to fondle the curling mass of hair that covered his chest, slowly working their way to his stomach. Finally, she pulled his shirt free and undid the final button.

He had remained passive under her ministrations, but now he reached over and slid the narrow straps of her nightie down and slipped her arms free. With eyes warm with desire, Zack drank in the sight of her full, firm breasts, their nipples hard and erect with hunger for him. He cupped them in his strong, male hands, then leaned over to kiss each one in turn with gentle reverence. Then he slid his arms around her back to pull her against his chest, his mouth seeking hers in a deep, draining kiss.

Lesley's hands tangled in the dark silken hair of his head, then moved down the strong column of his neck and pushed aside his shirt. His skin was velvet over the hard, firm muscles of his shoulders as she stroked him. Zack raised his head and grinned down at her.

'We got side-tracked,' he said. Standing up, he shrugged off his shirt and tossed it aside. With feminine appreciation, Lesley watched the play of his muscles as he reached for his belt buckle. 'Enjoying the show?' he teased, unfastening his belt and pulling it free from his trouser loops.

She tilted her head saucily, and looked at him consideringly. 'I guess you'll do . . . for a man your age.'

He gave her a look of mock affront and held the belt up threateningly. 'I ought to use this on you to teach you a little respect for your elders.'

She grinned back at him. He'd set the belt aside, and was unhooking the snap of his jeans when her gaze was drawn to a spot of light behind him. It was the reflection of the table-lamp off the glass covering the photo on the television set.

She stared at it, a cold chill creeping over her. It was Mandy's school picture. Her daughter, for whom she'd always tried to set a good example. Her daughter, who was upstairs right now, asleep, or at least supposed to be. Mandy had woken and come down once this evening already, she could again.

Hastily, Lesley reached for her robe and pulled it around her. In the process of unzipping his jeans, Zack was arrested by her action. 'What's the matter?'

'We can't, Zack.' She stood up and cinched the

belt of her robe tightly about her waist, hoping it would hold up her nightgown until she got upstairs.

His expression of confusion was tinted with irritation. 'This isn't very funny, Lesley.'

'I'm not trying to be funny. We can't, I can't let you make love to me.'

His dark eyes, moments ago warm and passionate, glittered with cold anger as he looked at her. 'I don't know what kind of game you think you're playing, but I'm not the man to play it with. Don't blow hot then cold with me,' he advised harshly.

He took a step towards her and she slipped past him to the other side of the room. Turning to face him, she said , 'I told you before I didn't want an affair with you.'

'That isn't exactly the message you've been giving me over the past half-hour. What changed your mind all of a sudden? You never used to be a tease.'

She saw the hard, angry set of his jaw, the expression of contempt in his eyes. She ran her hand distractedly through her hair, encountering tangles, and felt a moment's panic. Zack was furious with her and might forget about keeping his voice down. If Mandy walked in on them now . . .

'Look, Zack, I don't do this kind of thing,' she said, trying to keep her voice placating. 'I don't sleep around, and especially not when my daughter's upstairs in the same house.'

He gave her a look of disbelief. 'Good lord, woman, she's my daughter too. *We*, the *two* of us, are her parents. I'll admit it would be embarrassing if she walked in on us, but surely she's figured out we've done this at least *once* before . . . or have you totally neglected to tell her the facts of life?'

'She knows the facts of life,' Lesley retorted hotly, then realised how loudly she'd spoken. She lowered her voice, but it was still angry. 'I don't think at her age she needs to be acquainted with them first-hand, though. Besides that, how am I supposed to instil good moral values in her if she finds out I've been sleeping with you?' She could see he was about to say something, and rushed on, 'I know we *were* married, we had a child, but we're not married now.'

He looked totally exasperated. 'What the hell's got into you? When did you turn Quaker? We weren't married the first time you went to bed with me.'

'That was a totally different situation, and you know it. We were in love, we were planning to marry even though we anticipated things. If Mandy were to find out about us now, how am I going to explain to her that it's just sex, no emotional commitment, just a good time?'

She turned away from him so he wouldn't see the tears gathering in her eyes. It wasn't just Mandy she would have to explain things to, but herself as well. The words she had spoken echoed and re-echoed in her head—*sex, no emotional commitment*. How could she accept him on those terms and not want to die when he left her? She still loved him. If they slept together, it wouldn't be just sex without emotion for her. It would be a commitment on her part. She'd given him up once, she knew the emotional hell she had endured afterwards. She couldn't go through that again.

He had remained silent, so she took a deep breath to steady herself enough to speak. 'You want an affair. Well, I don't,' she said flatly.

A long minute ticked by, then he moved. He crossed the room to her in long, forceful strides, his hard hands catching her shoulders and swinging her around to face him. His fingers bit cruelly into her flesh as he looked down at her. She quelled beneath the fury in the gaze he raked over her. 'So it's blackmail, is that it?'

'I—I don't know what you're talking about,' she stammered.

'Don't you?' he jeered. To her relief, though, he dropped his hands and went over to pick up his shirt. He shrugged it on, not looking back to her until he had it buttoned. His eyes shone with contempt. 'You're not very original, Lesley. Eve probably pulled this trick on Adam. Put a ring back on your finger, and I get to share your bed. Are those your terms?'

'I didn't mean anything at all like that, and you know it!' she sputtered.

He ignored her rebuttal. 'I guess now I know *why* you haven't slept with your boyfriend. He won't come up to scratch, eh? So now you've decided to make me an offer!'

Lesley's mouth moved convulsively as she tried to unstick the words that were blocked in her throat by rage. Zack's gaze slid over her, derisive, contemptuous. Then he met her eyes, smiling sarcastically. 'I'll think about it.' Retrieving his belt and jacket, he walked out of the house.

CHAPTER SEVEN

THE NEXT morning, Lesley didn't go downstairs until it was almost time for her to leave for work. With Zack there, she had temporarily cancelled her arrangement with the Sheppards to look after Mandy every morning. He was able to get her ready for school and supervise her until the school bus picked her up. As he had taken over the morning chores as well, the only things she had to do before work was get herself ready to go and have breakfast. She decided to skip the meal today and beg a piece of toast from the cook when she got to the café. After last night, she didn't want anything to do with Zack. She just hoped he would take her at her word and leave the farm as she had asked him to.

Both he and Mandy were in the kitchen when she walked into the room.

'Gee, Mom, you're going to be late for work if you don't hurry,' Mandy advised, grinning. She was the one who was usually chided to hurry every morning. 'Daddy's keeping your breakfast warm in the oven.'

Lesley had avoided looking at Zack since she entered the room. Now, her eyes flicked to where he was sitting at the table with Mandy drinking coffee. As he stood up, she quickly looked away again, her face set. Who did he think he was—Mr Mom? She'd rather he spent his time packing instead of cooking her breakfast.

Zack went to the stove and bent down to take out a plate of eggs and bacon from the oven. As he straightened with it, Lesley looked pointedly at the wall clock. 'I'm running late. I'll grab something at work.'

Her daughter's mouth was filled with toast, but it didn't stop her from saying. 'But you always say we shouldn't leave the house in the morning without. . .'

'Don't talk with food in your mouth,' Lesley interjected curtly, then bit her lip at Mandy's startled look. 'I'm afraid I don't have time this morning,' she explained in a milder tone. She headed towards the door before her daughter could get down her mouthful of food and comment further. However, before opening it, Lesley hesitated. She just couldn't make herself walk out without knowing.

She turned back and looked directly at Zack. 'What time are you leaving?' As Mandy was with them, she tried to sound casual, but there was nothing casual in the hard glitter of her blue eyes. They met his and encountered a look as stony as her own.

He did smile though, a slow, taunting smile. Lesley held her breath as she waited for the answer to her question. 'I thought I'd drop Mandy off at school this morning to save her having to take the bus, then go on from there.'

The air in her lungs came out in a little whoosh. 'Fine, then.' She smiled, wondering why it was such an effort when she was having her own way. 'Have a safe trip,' she added politely, turning away and reaching out for the doorknob.

'Oh, I doubt I'll have any problems on a short

run into Greeley, especially as John will be doing the driving,' Zack said mildly from behind her.

Lesley swung back. 'Greeley?' she yelped.

Zack's eyes slid significantly to Mandy, who was momentarily engrossed in separating the yolk of her egg from the white. Lesley forced her features into a semblance of composure, but she couldn't subdue the angry flame in her eyes.

Her ex-husband grinned mockingly. 'Did I forget to tell you I arranged to go into Greeley with John Murray this morning to pick up some fence-posts for the corral? That back section is almost ready to fall down. I want to get it fixed before the horses break out and start tramping through John's corn. That wouldn't do them or the corn any good.'

Lesley's lips pressed into a tight line. If only Mandy would stop dawdling over her breakfast and leave the room! However, since her daugher seemed in no rush to finish her meal, Lesley knew she had to censor ninety per cent of what she'd like to say. What she *did* say was, 'I know the fence is in bad shape and I plan to get it fixed next autumn. I can't really afford to right now, so please don't bother with it—certainly not to the extent of letting it interfere with your *other* plans.'

'I haven't any *other* plans,' he came back meaningfully, watching the raging colour run up Lesley's cheeks. 'As for the cost, don't worry about it. I'll buy the posts . . . look on it as my contribution towards my board.'

Lesley was ready to forget they weren't alone. 'I——' she started, but he interrupted her.

'Hadn't you better be leaving? It's ten to six.'

Lesley treated him to a cutting look, then glanced at the clock. It usually took her fifteen minutes to drive to work, and it *was* ten to. Not saying another word, although her expression said quite a few, she turned away and slammed out of the house.

Lesley was late for work and it turned out to be one of those mornings when half the state of Colorado appeared to have decided to eat breakfast at the Columbine Café. She didn't even have time to gulp down a cup of coffee between taking orders and doling out food, let alone eat anything. Consequently, by the time the rush was over at nine o'clock, she was feeling pretty shaky. Disregarding what Estelle might say about her taking her meal break immediately instead of later in the morning when a third waitress came on shift, Lesley asked Clarence, the cook, to fix her some pancakes.

She had just sat down with them at the end of the counter, when the other waitress came over to her.

'Oversleep this morning and miss your breakfast?' Estelle asked, a faint sneer in her voice. 'You looked tired out . . . must have been a tough night.'

Lesley ignored her, taking a sip from her cup of coffee instead of replying. She had been expecting Estelle to come up with some snide remark all morning, and supposed only the crush of customers had saved her from it until now. The older woman had been surly to her all day yesterday. Lesley wasn't sure whether it was because she had been annoyed by her taking so long on her coffee break, or whether she was simply jealous because Zack had paid her all the attention and none to Estelle. If it was the latter, Estelle was welcome to him. Lesley would even giftwrap him!

After a couple of minutes, during which the other

waitress didn't move away, Lesley remembered she had to go on working with her. Besides, she *was* tired out. She'd hardly slept the night before and had already had a confrontation with Zack this morning. The last thing she needed was to quarrel with her co-worker. She said, 'I was late getting going this morning so I missed breakfast.'

'Don't worry about it. If I had a husband like that sharing my bed, I wouldn't want to get up early, either.'

The bite of pancake in her mouth suddenly lost its flavour and tasted like cardboard. Lesley managed to swallow it, then reached for her coffee. She took a swallow, then said, 'Look, he's not my husband . . . he's my *ex*-husband. And he doesn't share my bed, either!'

'Well, I guess you'll just have to keep trying, then,' Estelle advised flippantly, starting to turn away.

Something snapped in Lesley. Her hands trembling, she slammed her coffee-cup back on to the saucer, spilling half of it. She glared at the older woman through the moisture suddenly filming her eyes. 'I don't want to try . . . I don't have to try! He's the one who wants the affair. Now, can't you mind your own damn business and leave me alone?' A tear broke free and slid silently down her cheek. Seeing Estelle's startled look, Lesley hastily turned her head away and fretfully rubbed her cheek with her fingertips. More tears were joining the first, though, thwarting her attempts to disguise the fact that she was crying.

Crying! She was a grown woman with a daughter! How could she be so juvenile? she thought, swallowing the sob that was rising in her throat. She could sense Estelle hovering over her uncertainly. Unfortunately, not even the embarrassment of having an audience to her distress seemed to affect the tide of tears flowing from her eyes.

'Oh, honey, don't . . . I'm sorry,' Estelle stammered in distress, awkwardly patting Lesley's shoulder. 'Please, come on, calm down. I shouldn't have needled you, it's all my fault . . .' She sounded near tears herself.

'I'm sorry, Estelle,' Lesley choked, wondering if she would ever be able to stop crying now that she'd started. 'It's not your fault.' An awkward silence ensued, punctuated by Lesley's self-conscious sniffles. Finally, after several moments had lapsed, Lesley dared to look at her companion, hoping to find a smile for her.

As soon as Estelle saw her co-worker's tear-ravaged face, her arms went around her and she cradled her to her bosom. 'You poor kid. I'm sorry I was such a bitch to you. It's your old man, isn't it? Is he giving you a hard time?'

It was funny, really. Estelle was about as different from her mother as two women could be. Yet, when she put her arms around Lesley, it was like those times in childhood when her mother had comforted her through the little hurts and travails all youngsters go through. Lesley nodded against the soft, perfumed warmth of Estelle's bosom, and suddenly found she was spilling out the whole story of what a horrid mess her life had got into since Zack had come back into it.

The older woman let her talk it all out, and only when Lesley had been quiet for several moments did she drop her arms from around her. She gave her a bracing smile. 'You know, a couple of people have come in and they're giving us some awfully funny looks. How about you go wash your face now, and I'll go give them coffee?' OK?'

Lesley nodded somewhat sheepishly. Now that her control was returning, she felt unable to meet the other woman's eyes. Even though they had worked together for months, she and Estelle were practically strangers. She couldn't believe that she had bared her soul to her.

As Lesley turned to slide off her stool, Estelle touched her shoulder. 'Don't worry about what you told me being spread around. I won't blab to anyone.'

At the note of shy reaching-out in the waitress's voice, Lesley's embarrassment evaporated. She looked back at her, offering a smile that wasn't the least bit forced. 'I know you won't.

There was a subtle change in the atmosphere between them when Lesley got back from the cloakroom, and it lasted throughout the rest of the working day. Instead of two women who simply did their jobs in the same establishment, trying to stay out of each other's way, they were now pulling together, helping each other and . . . being friends.

At the Columbine, as in most restaurants, each waitress was responsible for taking care of her own section of tables. Prior to today, each of them looked after their own customers and pretty much ignored what went on in the other one's 'station'. Now, though, when Estelle had an extra moment, she took the coffee-pot around to re-fill the cups of the customers sitting in Lesley's section as well as her own. At lunch, when Estelle got a little behind clearing the dirty dishes from her tables, Lesley took a moment to clean them for her. That kind of co-operation made working with each other much more enjoyable.

However, when they were both finished work for the day and Estelle suggested they sit out front for a few minutes and have a soft drink together, Lesley was reluctant to agree. While she appreciated the new understanding between them, she was basically a very private person and not given to wholesale exchanges of confidences. If she hadn't been so upset that morning, she knew she would never have opened up to anyone, not even long-time friend like Betsy, about the situation with Zack.

Noting Lesley's hesitation, Estelle said quickly, 'Oh, I guess you have to get home to your little girl. Maybe some other time, then.'

There was a reserve in Estelle's manner now, and Lesley knew that the ground they had gained in their relationship was rapidly slipping away. She didn't want that to happen, so when the other woman turned to go Lesley said quickly, 'Please, I'd love to have a drink with you.'

'Are you sure it's OK? You haven't anything else you should be doing?' the older woman asked cautiously.

'No, I want to.' Lesley smiled at her. 'The school bus won't drop Mandy off for another hour or so. I'm not in any rush . . .' Estelle still didn't look convinced, so she added, 'To tell you the truth, I really don't want to see Zack alone.'

The older woman gave her a look of understanding as she nodded and they went to sit down. Once seated, with iced glasses of Pespi in front of them, Estelle said, 'I think I know how you feel. I don't know what I'd do if my ex turned up again.'

'I didn't know you'd been married,' Lesley said, a quiver of guilt niggling her conscience. They'd been working the same shift for months, and she knew nothing about Estelle's personal life. She suspected it was her fault, too. Although she'd always been polite to the other woman, she hadn't taken any pains to get to know her. If Lesley had just given her an opening before, they could very well have become friends right from the beginning.

'I was married for twelve years,' Estelle explained. 'He's a dentist. I worked in restaurants from the time we got married, helping to put him through school, then set up his practice. It was just starting to show a little profit when he ditched me for some college kid who came to him to have her teeth capped.' She gave Lesley a cynical smile that was at odds with the hurt vulnerablility that shone in her eyes. 'I expect that bastard would have dumped me before then, if he hadn't needed me to pay the bills.'

'I really am sorry, Estelle,' Lesley offered kindly.

She shrugged. 'It doesn't matter now. There's lots of fish in the sea.' She grinned. 'I know, I've fried a few of them. Let's talk about something else. Tell me about your little girl. I've always liked kids.'

Lesley complied, but in the back of her mind she was turning over what Estelle had said about her ex-husband. It explained a lot about the woman's character. She wasn't 'man-hungry' so much as unsure of herself as a woman. She needed the attention of the men who came into the restaurant as reassurance of her attractiveness as a woman.

However, Lesley suspected Estelle needed and wanted women friends just as much as she did men. Unfortunately, her behaviour with the opposite sex had an off-putting effect on the women she encountered. It was really too bad, Lesley thought, especially since, as she was beginning to discover, Estelle was quite a nice person when you looked beneath the surface.

Over the next few days, Lesley found she was grateful for her new friendship with her co-worker. With a sensitivity that Lesley would never have credited her with previously, Estelle never probed for information on what was happening with Zack. However, the knowledge that her new friend knew the whole story and was there to confide in if things started getting on top of her again made coping with her ex-husband's continuing presence much easier. For, of course, although she'd asked him to leave, he hadn't.

Until Thursday.

She arrived home that day just seconds before the school bus dropped Mandy off in front of their house. As she drove her middle-aged Honda Civic into the yard, she noticed Zack's pick-up camper wasn't parked in its usual spot over by the barn. However, as his accommodation was also his transportation, she didn't think much about it, particularly as Mandy didn't seemed concerned about her father's absence. Her daughter didn't remark on it, and once her afternoon snack had been consumed she went off to ride Sugar.

As supper time approached, however, Lesley started to get annoyed with her ex-husband's disappearance. Zack had taken his meals with them since his arrival. He wasn't *obliged* to eat with them, Lesley reminded herself; however, common courtesy dictated that if he were going to be late or miss a meal, he let her know. She had half a mind to just cook something for herself and Mandy, and let him fend for himself when he finally did show up.

Nevertheless, when she called Mandy in to eat, there was a huge bowl of spaghetti and meatballs sitting on the table. She told herself it was only because, while she was about it, she might as well fix enough to freeze the leftovers to serve another night. The surplus wasn't for Zack, although she supposed it could be reheated fairly easily if he hadn't had a chance to eat while he was out.

She and Mandy were seated and the meal started, when she realised her daughter still hadn't commented on Zack's absence. That was a bit odd—unless she knew where he was.

'Before you left for school this morning, did your father say anything to you about going somewhere today?' Lesley asked.

Mandy kept her eyes trained on her plate as she diligently cut a meatball in two, then speared one half with her fork.

'Mandy, did you hear me?'

The girl nodded, then said reluctantly, 'Some lady called him this morning and he said he'd have to be away for a couple of days.' She stuffed the meatball in her mouth and started to chew it with excruciating thoroughness.

Lesley's own meal was forgotten as her fork remained suspended in mid-air. Her eyes were trained on the place at the table where Zack usually sat. How empty it was! She'd told him to leave; she should be filled with joy that he'd finally done as she wanted. So why did she suddenly feel like crying? Why did the whole house seem filled with a huge, hollow silence just because one of its occupants, an unwelcome one at that, was no longer there?

Catching Mandy eyeing her curiously, Lesley forced herself to resume the meal. Placing a forkful of spaghetti in her mouth, she chewed it automatically, then found she had trouble swallowing it past the lump that had formed in her throat. Zack had left, but not only that, he'd gone to another woman. It must be his girlfriend—she must be pretty special, too, since he'd gone running to her the moment she beckoned.

'Is there something wrong with the spaghetti?' Mandy asked.

Lesley started and looked over to her daughter, then down at her plate. She'd forgotten about eating again. There was a hard ball of pain in her stomach, though, that made her think she'd be sick if she tried to eat another bite.

'It . . . it's the sauce,' Lesley improvised. 'I don't think I care for this brand. It isn't as good as the kind I usually buy, so I don't think I'll get it again.'

'I like it,' Mandy said, taking up another bite and shoving it into her mouth. Errant strands of pasta brushed red streaks down her chin.

'Well, I don't,' Lesley snapped in sudden irritation. Standing abruptly, she picked up her plate and took it to the counter to clean it off into She-Ra's bowl. She glanced back at Mandy and saw the child watching her with wide, bewildered eyes, and felt a wash of shame sweep over her. There was no need to take out her black mood on her daughter.

'Look, when you've finished, why don't we go over to Platteville and buy ourselves an ice-cream cone for dessert?'

Mandy's face brightened, the clouds dispersing. 'Super! Can I have a double-decker?'

'I don't see why not,' Lesley said, turning away

to stare out of the kitchen window. She couldn't see the barn from there, but knew there was a big, empty space in front of it where Zack's rig had been parked.

The members of Mandy's horse club started arriving at the farm on Saturday morning around ten. Several of the youngsters brought their horses, so the yard was soon filled with pick-ups, horse-trailers, and milling animals and people. Lesley set Mandy to directing traffic, as she searched the crowd rather desperately for the leader.

She could kill Zack for getting her into this mess. She hadn't even remembered that he had invited the group over for a session of roping and barrel-racing until the first pick-up towing a trailer had pulled into the yard. She felt dreadful about having to tell them the event was cancelled at this late date. However, without Zack, she didn't know what she was supposed to do with all these kids. She didn't even know how to ride! Zack had been teaching her after they first got married, but then she'd got pregnant and . . .

Finally she spotted Fred Morrisby, the leader, over by the barn directing the unloading of a pinto mare from a green horse-trailer. As she started across to him, a horn blared and she looked behind her. John's green Dodge pick-up had just turned into the drive and was coming towards her. Lesley stepped back out of the way, gaping at the vehicle. It wasn't towing a horse-trailer, but the box was filled with baby goats and a couple of white-faced calves.

When it halted beside her and John had climbed down from the driver's seat, she went over to him.

Before she could speak though, he said, 'We're going to have to get some of these vehicles out of the way so I can drive these fellas around the back of the barn and unload.'

Lesley drew her disbelieving stare away from the goats—*goats*!—and stared at John. 'Where did you get them?'

'Zack had me pick them up at the auction for him,' the farmer said, moving to go talk to the driver of a tan trailer that was blocking the pick-up's way.

Lesley caught up to him. 'You mean he *bought* them?'

'Sure. The kids need something to practise roping and tying,' John explained matter-of-factly. Lesley was still recovering from the shock of discovering this new way her ex-husband had found to waste his money, when they reached the driver of the trailer. John said to him, 'How about pulling your vehicle over there so I can get through? I need to get that around back of the barn.' He gestured to his truck and, at the other man's nod, started back towards it. 'Why don't you get the path clear for me, while I get moving again, Lesley? And watch those kids, I don't want to run over one of them.'

Lesley caught his arm, forcing him to halt. She gave him a look of utter frustration. 'Look, Zack isn't even here.'

'That's OK. He called me last night and said he would probably be a little late. Told me to go ahead and get set up without him.'

Lesley's mouth tightened. She supposed it would have been expecting a little too much of her ex-husband to have called *her* and told *her* what was going on. After all, this was only her farm, she only lived here, whereas he was the star boarder! He hadn't bothered telling her he was leaving—why should he put himself out telling her he was coming back?

John started away again, and again she stopped him. She was frowning. The horse corral was to the side of the barn. At the back of the barn there had been another corral at one time, but even when her dad was alive it had been little more than a ruin. All that was left were a few rotted posts and a lot of weeds. Beyond it was cultivated land. The hayfield was fenced, but surely . . .

'You can't turn those animals loose in that field behind the barn, John. The first cutting of alfalfa on it will be ready in another month. They'll bloat on it and trample what they don't eat.'

John gave her a look that clearly said, I'm not that stupid. 'I don't mean the hay field. I'll put them in the pen Zack built earlier in the week. Haven't you been out to look at it? Didn't Zack tell you about it?'

'He only said he was going to fix the horse corral.'

'Well, when you get these people out of my way, you can go look at the new one. Personally, I want to get these critters unloaded before noon,' John said impatiently, shaking her hand off his arm and striding over to the cab of the truck. As he swung himself behind the wheel, Lesley treated him to a final look of asperity and stalked away to do as he'd told her.

CHAPTER EIGHT

HER ex-husband had been busy while she'd been away at work all week, Lesley thought sardonically. Zack—knowing him, assisted by a crew of twenty-dollar-an-hour tradesmen—had erected a completely new corral and chute system on what had been a wasteland in back of the barn. Where once there had only been ragweed and thistles, some weathered wooden boards and a few broken down posts, a large professional-looking arena now stood. At one end of it, there were a couple of small enclosures that could be used as roping chutes, with a slightly larger pen behind to hold stock.

She hadn't had an opportunity to speak to Zack since his arrival a few minutes after John's. Perhaps that was just as well, she thought, her eyes drifting back to the new enclosure. With all these people around, it wasn't the best time to tackle him about the money he had been throwing around lately. The arena was made of manufactured metal panels and was the kind of system that could be erected quickly and with a minimum of labour. However, it was also a very expensive method of building a corral—especially when she really didn't need another corral on the farm. Lord knew how much he'd paid for it. It didn't sweeten her feelings towards him that he'd also been spreading his cash around in other ways as well. When she'd tried to pay John the money she owed him for the corn seed he'd planted, he told her

Zack had already paid him.

Whether her ex-husband could afford to spend money like water—although the thought that he couldn't was ever with her—really wasn't the point. He had no right to interfere in her life that way. During his absence these past few days, it had come home to her just how quickly he had insinuated himself into her life again. She'd missed him. She'd missed having another adult to talk to in the evenings, someone to discuss the day's activities with, to give advice, help her raise Mandy.

But he *wasn't* part of her life any more. She'd been independent of him for a long time, and the more he intruded into her existence now, the worse it was going to be when he left for good.

Her eyes went to the rangy man astride his chestnut gelding, Clancy, in the centre of the arena. Zack was supervising the group of youngsters as they attempted to tie up the legs on several baby goats. From the baas filling the air, the goats weren't too happy about the operation.

However, before Lesley could feel too sorry for the little animals, a small buck who'd managed to escape came hurtling back into the fray. Head down, the kid charged the rear end of one the boys who was stooped over a second goat, inexpertly trying to wrap a leather thong about its legs. The youngster went sprawling, his action having a domino effect when he lurched into the lad next to him, who in turn went off balance and into the next child.

Suddenly, it was the children who were lying in the dust of the arena and the little goats who had the upper hand. They took advantage of it by instituting a hilarious game of tag with the red-faced children that lasted a good fifteen minutes. It only ended when Zack ordered the children out of the arena and Clancy took charge. They then rounded up the unruly animals and herded them into a smaller pen where there was less scope for high jinks.

The show over, Lesley started to turn away. Most of the families of the club members were staying for the day, and had brought food for a pot-luck lunch. A couple of the mothers were organising things and had stressed that they didn't want her going to any trouble on their account. Just inviting them over for the day was enough of a contribution.

However, since Lesley hadn't actually been the one to invite them, and, as she hadn't known about it, hadn't prepared anything for the pot-luck either, she felt she ought to find some way of helping ensure the success of the day.

Before she could go, though, Fred Morrisby came up to her. 'It's really great of you and your husband to have us out here today.' Lesley grimaced. It was on the tip of her tongue to correct him—Zack was her *ex*-husband—but she refrained. It would be a waste of breath. Several people today had already referred to Zack as her husband, and correcting them had only earned her some strange looks.

'It's not often that the kids have an opportunity to learn from a real professional, and they're very grateful,' Fred continued.

'I'm sure my husband . . .' She broke off, appalled. Damn! Now *she* was doing it! Have *could* she have said that? He wasn't her husband and hadn't been for a long time. Why did poeple keep saying he was . . . why had she said it?

Of its own volition, her gaze sought out Zack. He'd backed Clancy into one of the roping chutes, and was coiling his lariat. He turned his head to speak to someone behind him, and Lesley studied his profile. Shaded by his cowboy hat, it stood out in stark relief against the lighter background of the sky and looked hard and uncompromising. He had a firm jawline, a straight, no-nonsense nose, a sparseness of flesh covering his facial bone structure that precluded handsomeness. But she couldn't see his eyes at this distance. They could be as hard and uncompromising as the rest of his face at times. But she'd seen them at other times—warm with sympathy, lit with laughter, burning with desire. Her husband . . .

Besides her, Fred interrupted her thoughts. 'Zack must be going to give us a demonstration. He'd said he didn't think he should because of his leg, but the kids must have talked him into it.' He moved forward to rest his arms on top of the railing of the arena.

Disturbed, Lesley followed him. She should have realised that was what Zack was planning: the tension in his expression: Clancy, alert and coiled to spring from the chute after the calf. She stared at her ex-husband's crippled leg. The damn fool.

A moment later, a calf shot out into the arena with Zack's big quarter-horse hard after him. The lasso snaked out and, as the loop settled over the calf's head, Clancy tucked his haunches under him, sliding to a stop. Zack was already half out of the saddle, and Lesley saw the spasm of pain cross his features as he landed on his game leg. It didn't stop him from running down the taut rope to the calf and throwing it to the ground, though. In a little more than an instant, he'd wrapped the pigging string around three of its legs and secured it with a 'hooey'. Then he raised his hands, stepping back from the tied animal.

Lesley stared at his face, unable to tear her eyes from the expression of triumph it held. He moved a couple of paces, and the unevenness of his gait told its own story of the pain he was in. However, his expression never altered but stayed with him as he called Clancy over and swung himself on to the saddle.

That look on his face despite his pain . . . *He loves his damned ole rodeo as much as he loves me.* The line from the old song haunted her as she watched Zack ride out of the arena. Eleven years ago, that was what a good part of it had been all about—their separation, the divorce. She'd been so young, so childish. She felt diminished every time she'd seen just how much he loved the rodeo, the competition, the challenge. She'd wanted him to give it all up to prove that he loved her.

Now, as she witnessed the satisfaction in his face after a successful run, the sheer joy, she felt ashamed of herself. Zack had loved his career. She'd been eaten up with jealousy for that other mistress in his life, and had wanted him to choose between them—and when he wouldn't choose, she'd made the choice for him.

Once through the gate, Zack rode Clancy up to where she was standing with Fred Morrisby.

Fred congratulated him. 'That was amazing.'

Zack's mouth twitched wrily. 'I'm too slow nowadays to be in the money. Once those kids get the hang of it, they'll leave me in the dust.' Despite his words, his eyes glowed with satisfaction.

'Well, you looked pretty good out there to me.' Fred glanced over to where a couple of the younger girls were struggling with a fifty-gallon drum. 'I think I'd better go help those two get the barrels set up,' he explained, walking away.

Looking down at Lesley from atop his horse, Zack grinned at her. 'Well, what do you think, old girl? Was I amazing or just an old man showing off?'

He was still riding high with elation over the run. He loved the rodeo and he always would. She shouldn't have tried to change him. She could see that now with a clarity that she never had those many years ago.

However, the lectures of her late parents still haunted her. It wasn't a life to share with a wife and family. They *had* been right. The rodeo was a harsh mistress that demanded more than a wife could accept, Lesley thought, her eyes going to his leg. He hadn't walked from the arena, but ridden the gelding. He didn't dismount now, either, and she wondered if it was because he couldn't. Damned fool.

'How's your leg?' she asked sharply.

His grin faded. As he took in her tight-lipped expression, his eyes frosted over. 'I guess I should have been prepared for your answer when I asked the question. So you think I was just an old man making a fool of himself by showing off,' he said grimly.

'You were a fool to risk damaging your leg,' she retorted, her sudden anger somehow making his disability easier for her to bear. She had to be angry. She couldn't let him know that it broke her heart that the rodeo he had so loved had punished him so. 'Fred told me that you originally weren't going to do a run, that it might be dangerous to your leg. You went ahead and did it, though. What if you'd landed on it wrong and done something so that you couldn't even walk at all? You were a fool to risk that!'

'So what if I'd hurt it? What's it to you, my dear *ex*-wife? You took yourself out of my life five years ago and you lost the right to take me to task over anything when you divorced me.' With a jerk on the reins, he wheeled Clancy away, leaving Lesley to stare after him, tears of hurt slowly clouding her vision.

Lesley spent Sunday afternoon in the kitchen engaged in a marathon baking session. Outside it was a beautiful day, the temperature up to eighty and not one cloud marred the perfect blue of the sky. However, Zack was out there with Mandy, and since yesterday the atmosphere between her and her ex-husband had been dead winter. It was wiser to stay inside and out of his way.

However, when she glanced out of the window and saw he had taken the camper off the back of his pick-up, she knew she'd have to go and talk to him, cold war or no. As long as his bed had wheels on it, he was a transient visitor who could leave at the turn of an ignition key. Setting the camper up on its own implied a permanence she wouldn't tolerate.

She waited until she saw Mandy go into the barn, then removed her apron and walked out of the house to where Zack was crouched down to adjust one of the camper supports.

'Zack?'

He looked up at her, then slowly stood. 'Lesley?' he mocked.

Lesley moistened her lips nervously. She couldn't help but recall what had happened last time she'd asked him to leave. 'You've taken the camper off the pick-up.'

'I'll give you full marks for observation.' Folding his arms, he leaned nonchalantly against the side of the camper, the smile on his lips taunting.

She pressed hers together angrily. 'How long are you planning to stay?'

'You keep asking me that. I'm beginning to think you don't like having me around.'

'Then I'll give *you* full marks for observation,' she snapped, flinging his words back at him. Although he appeared merely amused by her display of temper, there was an undercurrent of intractability about him that made her cautious. She forced her temper down. They needed to talk rationally about this. 'Mandy's been invited to go camping in Rocky Mountain National Park with Tina and her parents over Memorial Day weekend. They're leaving this Friday and she won't be back until late Monday night. When she's gone, you've no reason to be here.'

'Haven't I?' Starting at her feet, his eyes did a slow journey up her form. They followed her slim legs, encased in tight jeans, to her hips, her waist. She could almost feel his touch as his gaze lightly caressed her full breasts beneath her form-fitting T-shirt, then came to rest on her mouth. Lesley swallowed hard, trying to quiet the clamouring of her senses, aroused by his purely sexual appraisal.

She found her voice. 'You'll leave on Friday. I finish working for the restaurant until autumn then, too, and I don't want you around when I'm home all day.' He appeared unimpressed, his eyes continuing their leisurely survey of her body. 'There's . . . there's no reason for you to stay,' she added, slightly desperate. If only he would stop looking at her like that!

A slow smile spread over his features, but it didn't

reach his eyes. They were dark brown slate and held pure determination. 'With Mandy gone, you won't be able to use her as an excuse, will you?'

'I'm not going to sleep with you, Zack,' she vowed shakily.

His dark brows arched into peaks as he gave her a look of sceptical amusement. 'Don't you want to?'

'No, I don't!'

He considered her for a moment, watching the colour fluctuate in her face until it faded to the shade of skimmed milk. 'You know I'd never force you, so what's the problem? It shouldn't bother you if I stick around next weekend whether Mandy's here or not. I've got my camper. You'll have that big comfy double bed in your room all to yourself.' His thrust hit home—at one time they had shared that bed— and he turned the knife slowly. 'Tell me, how are the slats holding up? You know what I mean. I'm sure you remember the time one broke and dumped us and the mattress on the floor. We were lucky it didn't wake us out of a sound sleep . . . but then, I guess if we had been sleeping, it wouldn't have broken.'

Afterwards, she wasn't sure what she would have replied to him had Mandy not returned at that moment, allowing her to end the conversation and escape back to the house. Lesley hadn't realised that she'd cherished so many precious memories of their life together until now when Zack took them out and used them as weapons against her.

The night the bed had broken stood out in her mind. It had been an awful shock to unexpectedly crash downward. She hadn't recovered from it when she'd experienced a swift stab of mortification because her parents couldn't help but to have heard the thump.

They wouldn't have needed much imagination to figure out what she and Zack had been doing to cause the bed to break. However, when Zack had started to chuckle, she had seen the funny side of it too. Burying themselves in the bedcovers, they'd muffled their peals of laughter as best they could.

And afterwards . . . Lesley looked down at her trembling hands. The perspiration that beaded her forehead had nothing to do with the heat in the kitchen. Afterwards, Zack had kissed her slowly and deliberately before making warm and delicious love to her.

She couldn't possibly spend the weekend alone with him!

Her eyes went to the wall telephone, and she crossed over to it and lifted the receiver. If he wouldn't leave, then she would.

Betsy answered the phone on the fourth ring. 'Hi, Betsy, it's me, Lesley.'

'Lesley! I haven't heard from you for ages. How are you doing?'

That was a tough question to answer over the telephone, so Lesley hedged and plunged into a spate of small talk that lasted several minutes. Finally though, she casually brought the conversation around to the purpose of the call. 'What with Mandy being away this coming weekend, I thought maybe I'd take a break too. Could you put me up for a couple of days?'

'Oh.' Her friend hesitated. 'Actually I'm not going to be here. I'm taking a few days off, too. I'm going to Las Vegas for the weekend.'

'I see,' Lesley replied. She thought feverishly, wondering what she could do now. Betsy lived in Cheyenne, a nice safe distance away, but most of her other friends lived in the neighbourhood of the farm, and it would look pretty odd if Lesley asked one of them to put her up for a few days.

Las Vegas . . . if she hadn't been so desperate to get away from Zack, she knew she'd never have considered it. However, she *was* desperate, and for once in her life she had extra funds. She had the money she was supposed to pay John for the corn seed. She'd intended making Zack take it, but . . .

'How would it be if I came with you?' she suggested impulsively. 'I've never been to Las Vegas and I've always been curious to see it.'

'Well . . .' Betsy answered slowly. 'I . . . er I'd love for us to do that some time, but I don't think this time . . .'

'Oh, don't worry about it,' Lesley inserted hastily 'You probably made your plans a long time ago, and I don't want to upset them.' She felt terrible for placing Betsy in an awkward situation. So much for giving in to the impulse to invite herself along.

There was an uncomfortable silence, then Betsy said, 'The truth is, I'm going on my honeymoon.'

'Honeymoon?' Lesley exclaimed, then fell abruptly silent. She was hurt. She'd always thought of Betsy as her best friend, even though they didn't see each other that often. Lesley would have thought she would have told her long before now that she was serious enough about someone to consider marrying. At the very least, she would have expected to be sent a wedding announcement.

Her friend explained gently. 'I've known him for years, but I've only been going out with him for a few weeks. I thought about telling you how things were heading with Matt when I first knew, but I didn't know how you'd react.'

Lesley was stung. 'Surely you know me better than that, Betsy! I'm very happy for you. Jerry's been gone a long time. I never imagined that you wouldn't remarry some day.'

'It's nothing to do with Jerry,' the other woman interrupted. 'At least, not the way you're thinking. I'm marrying Matt Carmichael.'

'Matt Carmichael?' Lesley echoed. It took a moment for her to place the name, and even then she couldn't believe it. 'You mean, Matt Carmichael the rodeo clown?'

'That's right.'

Being a rodeo clown wasn't the frivolous occupation that the title implied. Oh, they wore funny clothes and entertained the crowd with snappy patter and corny jokes. However, their real work was during the bull-riding event of the rodeo, when they were responsible for drawing the bull away from fallen riders. It was a highly dangerous occupation. How could Betsy even consider marrying someone who flirted with raging Brahma bulls for a living . . . especially after Jerry . . .

'Oh, Betsy!'

There was a wealth of feeling in those two words that came through clearly on the telephone wires. 'I know what you're thinking, Lesley, and that's why I didn't tell you before. I know how you feel about rodeo men, about the bulls, and I sort of feel the same way. But I love Matt. I'm not going to give him up because I don't like his job. Love comes along too seldom to throw it away.'

Lesley bit at her lower lip, not knowing quite what to say. There was a shade of accusation in her friend's tone, and she knew Betsy was thinking about her and Zack. For all that she was Lesley's friend, she was Zack's as well, and Lesley knew she had never approved of the way she had treated her ex-husband. She didn't want to get into it now, not on the phone, not when she was chafed raw by Zack's reappearance in her life.

'Have you asked him to give up the rodeos?'

'I wouldn't do that, Lesley. It's his life, it's too important to him. You know how it is with rodeo men, it's like an infection with them.' Lesley didn't respond. She couldn't argue with the other woman's statement. It *was* an infection, a disease that could be fatal. Betsy knew it too; she'd lost one husband, how could she take that risk again?

'Is Zack staying at the farm now?' Betsy asked quietly. Lesley wasn't surprised by the question. Somehow it seemed they had been talking about Zack all along. 'Is that why you want to get away for the weekend?'

'Yes.'

'Can't you give him another chance? I'm sure that he still loves you, and his riding in the rodeo isn't an issue any more.'

'It isn't that simple, Betsy,' Lesley replied wearily. 'I just . . . it's been too long.'

'Is it this Brian that you go out with? Are you in love with him?'

'Brian?' Now Lesley was surprised. While she had flirted with the idea of moving her relationship with Brian on to a more serious plane, it had never been more than an idea . . . and not a very good one, either. 'There's nothing like that between us . . . we're just good friends.' She laughed at little, recognising the ambiguity of the cliché. 'You know what I mean. Actually, I think I see so much of him because he really gets along well with Mandy.'

'He does?' Betsy asked surprised. 'I thought she didn't like him.'

'She didn't tell you that, did she?' She adores him . . . she ought to, he'd spoil her rotten if I gave him half a chance.

'Oh, I guess I misunderstood her,' the other woman said thoughtfully. There was a few moments' pause, then she continued, 'Lesley, I'm sorry about the weekend. I'd invite you to the wedding, but we just plan to go to one of those little chapels on the Strip and do it. I didn't want any fuss, so we aren't having any guests.'

'I understand.' Lesley glanced over at the clock. The call to Cheyenne was long-distance and they'd been talking for over a half an hour. It might be wise for her to take a tranquilliser before she opened the next phone bill. 'I guess I'd better get off the phone,' she said. 'Good luck, Betsy, and I wish you all the best. Goodbye.'

Lesley gently replaced the phone receiver on the hook and stared at it thoughtfully for a moment. She found it hard to accept that Betsy would marry a man like Matt Carmichael after losing Jerry the way she had. Jerry had ridden the bulls and saddle-broncs. At his last rodeo, he had been close to making a qualified ride of eight seconds. An instant before the bell rang, though, he'd been tossed. In a flash, the Brahma had spun around and gored Jerry before the clowns could draw his attention away from the fallen rider. The scent of blood had driven the animal wild. After mauling Jerry's limp form, he'd charged the clowns. They'd managed to evade him, but they might not have.

And Matt Carmichael was a clown. Betsy had almost gone under when she'd lost Jerry. How would she survive losing another husband? How could she take that risk?

CHAPTER NINE

ON FRIDAY evening Lesley applied her lipstick, then stepped back from the mirror to inspect the results. The warm peach gloss toned well with her honey complexion, and the touch of teal eyeshadow she applied to her lids brought out the colour of her eyes. However, those eyes held a look of faint misgiving in their depths as she surveyed herself.

It wasn't caused by her dress, a summery cotton blend, with a V neckline and full skirt. She'd had it for a couple of years, but still liked it, especially the turquoise fabric splashed with huge white blossoms. The style hadn't dated and it was dressy enough for a restaurant without being too sophisticated.

So it wasn't her make-up or attire that was worrying her. Since she had been blessed with hair that 'behaved' itself that didn't concern her either. Worn loose this evening, it rippled in shining golden waves around her shoulders, making her look young and carefree.

None the less, that look was still with her when she picked up her evening-bag. She tried manfully to dispel it as she went downstairs. She might have a few qualms about her plans for the evening, but *anything* had to be better than spending it alone with Zack.

She pushed through the door into the kitchen before she realised the room was occupied. Zack was seated at the table, looking very much at home. At her entrance, he lowered the newspaper he had been reading and gave her a long look. His eyebrows shot up and he let out a low wolf whistle.

'Very nice!' he exclaimed. Laying the paper aside, he got to his feet. 'When you disappeared after Mandy left and didn't come back, I wondered what you wanted to do about supper.' He gestured to her dress. 'You look too pretty to be stuck over a hot stove. Give me a few minutes to get changed and I'll take you out to dinner.'

Casually dressed in close-fitting faded denims and a plaid western shirt rolled up to expose deeply tanned forearms, he was disturbingly attractive. The impact he would have dressed in more formal clothing didn't bear thinking about. As it was, Lesley could feel his magnetism beckoning to her. Dragging her eyes away from, she said quickly, 'I already have plans.'

Even after turning him down, she still had the urge to retract her words and do something stupid like accept his invitation. Maybe she should see a psychiatrist. The only reason she was dressed up and going out was to get away from him!

'So, your gallant knight has returned.' Zack broke the short silence that had fallen between them. Lesley glanced over to him and saw his smile had vanished.

It took her a moment to digest the meaning of his remark. In her surprise, she blurted out the truth. 'I'm going out with Estelle.' Afterwards, seeing his smile return, she knew she should have let him go on thinking she was going out with Brian. Betsy had seemed to think there was a lot more to Lesley's friendship with Brian than there really was. From his comments, she knew Zack thought the same thing. Maybe, if she reinforced the notion that she had another man in her life, her ex-husband would remember that *their* life together was over and leave her in peace.

'I didn't know that you were that friendly with her. Somehow, she didn't strike me as quite the type you'd pick to go with for a "girls' night out",' Zack commented.

That was true, Lesley admitted silently. Ever since Monday, when Estelle had suggested the outing and she had agreed to it. Lesley had been battling with misgivings. Estelle was a much nicer person than she had originally thought, and working with her at the café had been more enjoyable since their new understanding. However, given the other woman's attitude towards men, Lesley wasn't sure how a social evening with her would turn out. Lesley wasn't into 'cruising', and the idea of picking up some strange man to spend the evening with simply wasn't on as far as she was concerned.

She suddenly realised that Zack was watching her. He'd probably read every thought that had just passed through her head. 'We're just going out to dinner in Boulder,' she said defensively.

'And that's all?'

Lesley shot him an angry look. What she did with her evening was none of his business. Maybe Estelle *had* said something about going on somewhere else after their meal, but that didn't mean there was anything wrong in it. The other woman had just mentioned she'd like to introduce Lesley to a place called Billy the Kid's. Apparently there was an excellent country and western band playing there this weekend. Lesley wasn't naïve enough not to realise that Billy the Kid's was a nightclub, but that didn't mean they wouldn't be going there for the sole purpose of listening to the music.

'Look, Zack, if you want to give me the third degree, shouldn't you tie me to a chair and shine a bright light in my eyes? I told Estelle I'd meet her in the car park of the motel at seven. It's almost that now, so if you don't mind, I'll be going.'

She started across the room towards the hook by the outside door where she kept her car keys. Zack pre-empted her and reached them first. 'I haven't finished talking to you yet.'

'I'd like my car keys,' Lesley said tightly. Who did he think he was? She didn't question *him* about his activities! He'd done another disappearing act on Tuesday. He hadn't been home when she got back from work, and she hadn't seen him again until this morning. Naturally she was curious as to where he had gone . . . who the 'lady' on the phone was that seemed to have him at her beck and call. But did she snoop into his affairs? Did she demand answers? Of course not, and it just wasn't because she knew he probably wouldn't tell her anyway. As he had so succinctly reminded her the day of the rally, they were divorced. She had no right to comment on his life.

And he hadn't any right to comment on hers! Lesley glared at him with renewed venom.

He merely ignored her, still jangling the keys lightly in his hand. 'Are you driving your car over to Boulder?'

'You know, Zack, you aren't my husband any more. You have no right to question me. It's none of your damn business what I do.'

He gave her a sarcastic smile, then shrugged. 'If that's the way you feel about it.' He tossed the keys into the air, caught them and slipped them into his pocket.

Lesley gave him a furious look, inclined to be stubborn. However, he obviously wasn't going to relent, so finally she said sulkily,' 'We're taking Estelle's car to Boulder. It saves her driving all the way out here if I meet her at the Prairie Inn, though.'

'And where are you going after the restaurant?' he continued the inquisition.

There was nothing for it but to tell him. She'd watched the keys disappear into his pocket and knew they were as unreachable as if he'd sent them to the moon until he chose to give them back to her. 'Estelle suggested we go on to a place called Billy the Kid's. Satisfied?'

'Have you been there before?'

Lesley shook her head. 'Can I just have my keys?' she asked yet again.

He nodded, reaching into his pocket and retrieving the keys to hold out to her. Her hand shot out to take them from him, and he captured it in his. When she tried to tug it free, his fingers tightened and she could feel the hard callouses that covered his palms.

She looked up to meet his eyes, trying to inject fury into her own but having little heart for it. His own eyes were serious and curiously intent, softening her own. Close to him, her hand in his, she was too vitally aware of him to sustain other thoughts and emotions. 'I'll stick around the house tonight,' he said. 'You have any problems, you call me and I'll come get you.'

'What kind of problems?'

'You don't know what kind of place this Billy the Kid's is. You might decide you want to come home before Estelle. Or you might not want her driving you home if she has too much to drink.'

'I'm not a child, Zack,' Lesley protested, though there was no heat in her voice.

'I know, that's the problem.' He dropped his head and planted a firm kiss on her mouth, then stepped back from her. When he released her hand, the car keys stayed in her palm. 'Take care of yourself, now.'

Feeling confused, Lesley stared at him briefly, then down at the keys in her hand. She hadn't been keen on going before, but she'd wanted to get away from Zack. She felt even less like going now, and part of it was that now she wished she was staying home with Zack. She wished she'd stop being so schizophrenic!

She gave him one last look before turning to go out the door. He was a heart-stoppingly attractive man. She wondered if it would have made any difference to her feelings for him if he'd grown fat and bald during those years they'd been apart. Somehow, she didn't think it would. There was more to her ex-husband than just good looks.

However, she'd be a fool to change her mind about going out. It would be too dangerous. Besides, she'd promised Estelle, and her friend was probably already waiting for her in the car park of the motel.

They had been at Billy the Kid's for about half an hour, when Lesley excused herself from Estelle and went to the ladies' room. As she threaded her way through the tables towards the exit, she decided that her qualms about the evening had been unfounded. While Billy the Kid's was a nightclub, there was nothing sleazy about it. Although supposedly decorated as an Old West saloon, Lesley suspected that the furnishings were far grander than any establishment of those days had enjoyed. The walls were panelled in polished walnut that glowed in the light from the brass lamp scones. Tiffany lamps, turned low, hung over the tables in the centre of the room.

Near the end of the room, where she and Estelle were sitting, there was a postage-stamp dance-floor with music provided by a country and western band. Although they played loud enough to preclude conversation during their sets, that in itself was an advantage. She and Estelle had just about talked themselves out over dinner. At this stage of the evening, Lesley was content to sit quietly and listen to the music. She suspected that Estelle would have liked to have danced, but Lesley was rather relieved that no one had come up to ask them. She didn't want to give some stranger the opportunity of groping her on the pretext of dancing with her and, besides, she was tired. She had worked her usual eight hours at the restaurant that day and wasn't up to 'boogie-ing the night away'.

However, as there weren't many unattached males in the club, Lesley didn't expect that anyone would come over to them. With that thought in mind, she was slightly startled to see that Estelle was no longer alone when she returned to the table. Two men had joined her in Lesley's absence.

Lesley was eyeing the strangers with consternation, when Estelle spied her. 'Come on and meet Evan and Clark. It's a real piece of luck that we ran into them. I didn't know they'd be there tonight.'

Lesley managed to summon a smile from somewhere as she allowed the other woman to introduce her. At least Estelle seemed to have known the two men previously, so it wasn't quite the same as picking up a couple of strangers. However, as she suffered their inspection, Lesley didn't consider it 'a real piece of luck' that they were obviously expecting to spend what was left of the evening at their table. Evan, in particular, gave her the sort of look a thirsty man might bestow on a glass of water in the burning desert. Considering that, despite his modish dress, he still looked old enough to be her father, she wasn't flattered.

Every single one of her earlier misgivings about an evening out with Estelle came to roost over the next-hour. Clark and Estelle got up to dance after Lesley joined them, and it soon became apparent that they were good friends, *intimate* good friends. It was a slow, smoochy number, and, although the dance-floor was dimly lit, the gloom didn't conceal what was going on between the other two. They might have been Siamese twins, joined at the front from lips to knees.

Lesley watched them for a few minutes in silent embarrassment, then glanced over to her companion. Evan had been watching them as well, and he suddenly turned his head and met her look. He smiled. 'That looks like fun. Would you like to dance?'

She decided she didn't like Evan's smile. When he shifted his chair slightly so that his shoulder brushed hers as he leaned his elbows on the table-top, she decided she wasn't terribly fond of the rest of him, either. He was dressed in western garb, with a pearl-studded lavender satin shirt and tailored trousers. His belt sported a huge silver buckle adorned with a bucking bronc in raised relief. Noting his pudgy, soft hands as he fingered his glass, Lesley decided he was about as genuine as his 'alligator-skin' cowboy boots.

It was impossible not to mentally compare him with someone with Zack. She might have grown to hate the rodeos, but at least her ex-husband had been real. He was a rugged, outdoors man who wouldn't have been caught dead in a get-up like Evan's dandified cowboy outfit.

'So, what do you say?' her companion asked.

She realised he was still waiting for an answer to his invitation to dance. 'Er . . . no, thank you. I'm a little tired, I had to work today.'

She edged her chair back, increasing the space between them. Undeterred, he leaned closer. 'Where do you work?'

Lesley hesitated. It was bad enough having to spend time with Evan now, without having him turn up at the Columbine some day. Besides, if she told him she was a waitress, he was just the type to take that to mean she was fair game. Of course, Estelle might tell him that they worked together some time later, but then again, she might not. Lesley decided to take that risk. 'I'm a teacher,' she lied.

'Oh, really? I envy your pupils.' He grinned, scooting his chair a bit closer. Apparently, he considered teachers fair game as well. Lesley pointedly moved her chair farther away. If this kept up, they'd soon be out on the dance-floor without ever having left their seats!

Evan reached over and caught a strand of her hair between his thumb and forefinger. As he fondled it, he looked straight into her eyes and said, 'Your students are lucky to have a golden-haired goddess to instruct them. Care to give me a lesson?'

She'd love nothing better! She smiled sweetly into his bold eyes. 'I'm afraid my students don't appreciate my charms, but then they can't see much of them when I'm wearing my habit.'

Evan frowned slightly. 'Your what?'

'My habit. We're a very liberal order, though; we're allowed to wear street clothes outside the convent,' Lesley explained, then asked innocently, 'Didn't Estelle tell you? I teach in a convent. I'm going to become a nun.'

For an instant he gave her a hard look, then threw back his head and laughed. 'You've got a cute sense of humour, honey!' He slipped his arm around her shoulders and gave her a hug, then left his arm in place.

If her arm hadn't been trapped between her side and the arm of her chair, she would have given him a hard jab in the ribs with her elbow. She tried shrugging free of his hold, but he ignored her gesture. Looking around somewhat wildly for Estelle, she hoped to catch her eye and bring her to the rescue.

However, Clark and Estelle seemed to have disappeared from the dance-floor. Her eyes moving on towards the exit, Lesley froze.

Oh, hell, what was he doing here?

Not having a good time from the look of him. Lesley watched Zack weave his way through the tables towards them, his stride purposeful despite his limp, his face grim.

She'd almost forgotten about Evan sitting next to her—Evan with his arm around her. He'd followed her gaze. 'Who's that, Sister Lesley? Your Father?' he joked.

Zack had reached the table and heard the last question. 'I'm not her father, but you look old enough to be. I suggest you take your hands off my *wife.*'

Lesley gasped at her ex-husband's audacity. Meanwhile Evan snatched his arm from around her as though he'd suddenly discovered she had a contagious disease. Zack smiled at the other man then, but the hard aggression never left his eyes.

'She never said she was married,' Evan protested. 'She was feeding me some cock-and-bull story about being a nun.'

Zack's lips twitched, and as he slid a glance at Lesley she caught a glimmer of amusement thawing the cold anger in his eyes. It was back though when he returned his attention to Evan. 'And you're no respecter of the church? I think you should have taken the hint and buzzed off instead of mauling her.'

Evan looked affronted. 'It was a joke.'

'Well, the joke's over. You can take the hint now.'

The older man moistened his lips. His eyes moved from Zack to Lesley, then back again. Coming to a decision, he got to his feet, muttering something under his breath before stalking away.

Zack immediately appropriated his chair, sitting down and giving Lesley a long look. Suddenly he chuckled. 'A nun? Is that the best you could come up with?'

Lesley felt her cheeks flame with embarrassment and riveted her eyes on her drink glass. It hadn't been a particularly brilliant idea. After a moment, though, a grin started tugging at her mouth. 'He almost believed me,' she said, starting to laugh.

Zack's deeper tones joined with hers, and it took them a moment to regain their composure. When their mirth was once again under control, Lesley realised that Zack's arm was now around her, his head close to hers as he leaned towards her. Her flesh had crawled when Evan had held her in the same manner, but the little tingles racing up and down her spine now had nothing to do with revulsion. She averted her face.

'What are you doing here, Zack?'

'Checking up on you,' he admitted blithely. She threw him an indignant look and he grinned. 'Are you going to tell me you're not glad I showed up? Before you answer that, I'll tell you I was watching you trying to fend off your latest conquest for about five minutes before I came over. I'll leave again if you want me to. He's still over there, holding up the bar. He'll keep you from getting lonely.'

Lesley glanced towards the bar. Evan was watching her and Zack with a disgruntled expression on his florid features. She wouldn't put it past him to come back to the table if Zack left her alone. Consequently, when Zack slipped his arm from around her and started to push his chair back, she lay her hand on his wrist to forestall him. 'No, please, stay.'

Zack shrugged nonchalantly, but his smile was satisfied. 'If that's what you want.'

He hailed the waiter over and ordered a beer, accepting Lesley's refusal to have another drink. When the man had left, an awkward silence fell between them. Lesley made a pretence of watching the dancers, but when Zack had his drink, and still didn't seem to be going to say anything, she did. 'I don't know where Estelle is. She was dancing.'

'I think I know where she is.'

Lesley gave him a surprised glance. 'You do?'

'What kind of car does she drive?' Frowning slightly, she told him, and he nodded. 'She's outside in her car.'

'She is?' Automatically, Lesley picked up her bag. 'You mean she's ready to leave? She should have told me.'

'I don't think she's going any-where just yet.'

'Then what's she doing outside?' Lesley wanted to know. 'Maybe I should go check on her.'

Zack gave her an indulgent look. 'You know, you're still almost as naïve as you were the day I married you. Estelle isn't alone out there, and judging by the steam fogging up the windows, I don't think she'd like to be disturbed.'

'Oh . . . oh!' So Clark had taken Estelle out to her car for a necking session. Well, Lesley thought wryly, she supposed it was a little more private than the dance-floor. None the less she was embarrassed by her friend's behaviour, and studiously avoided looking in Zack's direction. She should never have accepted Estelle's invitation to come out with her tonight.

Seeing her discomfort and seeking to ease it, Zack reached over and touched her arm. 'Would you like to dance?'

Lesley hesitated briefly, then nodded. When he looked at her like that, she forgot that she'd been too tired earlier to dance. Dancing with him, being held in his arms, sounded like heaven. 'Yes, please.' With his hand under her elbow, he helped her to her feet.

'I'll warn you, I might not be much good at this,' he admitted as he led her to the floor. 'A slow two-step's about all I can manage these days.'

She'd forgotten about his leg. She looked down at it and said, 'Maybe we shouldn't dance, then.'

'I'll be OK,' he assured her, pulling her into his arms. 'I'm just not Fred Astaire.'

'Well, I never was Ginger Rogers,' Lesley said, laying her cheek against his chest. A slow shuffle around the floor would do. It was enough to feel his arms around her. As she relaxed against him, the spell of the music washed over them, encasing them in a magic circle.

CHAPTER TEN

LESLEY came home from Boulder with Zack. As he turned into the farm drive, the reflection from the truck headlights glinted across the darkened windows of the house. It seemed strange coming home to an empty house at this time of night. There was no babysitter waiting to go home, no need to be quiet to avoid awakening Mandy.

Maybe she'd been a fool to come with him. When Estelle had come back into Billy the Kid's with Clark and seen Lesley and Zack, she'd come flying over to them like an irate mother hen who'd discovered her only chick being stalked by a cat. Although she'd been only too willing to abandon Lesley to the company of Evan, her prejudice against ex-husbands caused her to place Zack into a different category altogether. She'd dragged Lesley off to the ladies' room for a pow-wow. Once there, Lesley had had considerable difficulty convincing her that she really did want to spend the rest of the evening with Zack. Finally, however Estelle had had no choice but to accept Lesley's assurances, and she left soon after with Clark.

As for the rest of the evening . . . Lesley sighed contentedly as Zack parked the pick-up by the barn. It had been *fun*. They had danced a little, talked a lot, laughed together. It had been almost like when they had first got married and life was theirs to enjoy and savour, and not worry over.

In the silent darkness of the vehicle, she could feel Zack's eyes on her and glanced in his direction. Perhaps if he had made a move towards her, pulled her into his arms, she might have reacted differently. However, when he simply reached down and released the catch of his seat-belt, then opened his door and slid from behind the wheel, she knew she didn't want the evening to simply end. Lesley watched him as he walked around the front of the truck to her side. He opened her door and reached out a hand to assist her down from the high seat.

Once out of the truck, Lesley hesitated, shifting nervously on her feet. By nature, she wasn't an impulsive person, and it wouldn't take much to cause her to chicken out. She usually thought out her every action well in advance. About the only time in her life she hadn't worked everything out beforehand had been when she'd married Zack. She'd thrown her bonnet over the windmill for him, leaving school, defying her parents.

Tonight . . . she glanced over to the vacant house. Mandy wouldn't be back until Monday night . . . Perhaps she gave life a little too much thought, worried a little too much about the future . . .

'Would you like to come into the house for a while?' she asked.

'If that's what you want,' he agreed after a long pause. He was still holding her hand, but, when he would have released it, her fingers clung to his. In the moonlight, Lesley was aware of his look, and averted her head as they started towards the house. Having made her decision, she felt suddenly shy.

Zack opened the door to the kitchen, reached in to switch on the light, before stepping to let her precede him. Once inside, Lesley stood uncertainly in the centre of the room, then turned to him. 'Should I make some coffee?' She gestured towards the stove, her hands fluttering like nervous butterflies.

Zack smiled and came to stand in front of her, netting her fingers in his. He looked down at her as she bent her head. Her lowered lashes cast lacy shadows across her smooth cheeks, her lips trembling slightly. 'You didn't ask me in for coffee, did you?' he asked gently.

Lesley shook her head. She was acting like an awkward seventeen-year-old, and yet that was how she was feeling. The mother of an eleven-year-old daughter, she was hardly a virgin, but she was filled with uncertainties. It had been a long time since Zack had made love to her.

With his thumb, he stroked the back of her hand in a soothing motion. Lowering his head, his lips brushed her temple then traced a line down the side of her face to the graceful curve of her neck. Lesley trembled and, releasing her hands, Zack slipped his arms around her and gathered her to him.

Her own arms stole up around his neck and she raised her face to his. She closed her eyes as his mouth swooped down to cover hers, her bones melting at the contact. There was no gentle swell to desire, but an instant upsurge of passion that rocked her to her foundations. Zack's reaction echoed hers and destroyed his attempt at tender wooing. His hands were firm and masterful as he caressed her with urgent insistence. Caught up in a potent upheaval of aroused emotion, Lesley arched against him, straining her hips to his thighs as he stroked her spine and buttocks.

His lips eased away from hers. 'You can't put me off this time. I won't wait for you any longer, darling,' he growled, his mouth sliding over her cheekbone to her ear. His hand found her breast and the warm weight of it filled his palm. She didn't want to put him off . . . she couldn't. Flames touched her skin, torching her to fiery need as his fingers brushed over the hard button of her nipple. A low whimper rose in her throat as the yearning for fulfilment reached fever pitch.

Zack swept her into his arms and carried her from the room to the foot of the stairs. He paused, taking her lips in a long, hungry kiss filled with ardent promise. Slowly easing her on to her feet, he let her body slide down the length of his. 'I'd never make it up the stairs carrying you,' he confessed, ruefully brushing his crippled leg with his hand.

Lesley stared up into his eyes, hers glowing in the darkened hall. 'It doesn't matter.' she breathed. Her arms were wrapped around his waist, and she reached up on her toes to touch his lips with hers. They met and held, threatening to run out of control. Zack groaned as he tore his mouth away.

'Come on,' he ordered gruffly as he slipped his arm behind her back and urged her up the stairs. Held close to his side, Lesley matched her steps to his as he led her to her bedroom.

Moonbeams streamed through the open curtains, flooding the room with pale light. As Lesley moved away from Zack to turn on the bedside light, he held her back. 'Don't,' he commanded, turning her to face him. Sliding his arms around her, his fingers sought out the back zipper of her dress. 'Your skin glows like marble in the moonlight. I want to see you . . . touch you and revel in your warm and fragrant flesh.'

He slipped the dress from her shoulders and it fell

to the floor in a swirling pool. With a deft movement, he dispensed with her bra, allowing her full, throbbing breasts to spill free. He ran his hands over their pulsating warmth, then down her waist to her hips to slide her silken panties down her thighs so that she could step out of them.

With impatient fingers, Lesley tugged at the front of his shirt, releasing the pearl snaps that held it closed. Pushing it off his shoulders, she moved foward until the tips of her breasts brushed against the warm, hair-covered expanse of his exposed chest, her arms encompassing his neck. The contact sent an electric current of sensuality arcing through her nerve-ends, and she shivered in anticipation.

Zack ran his palms over the smooth, baby-soft skin of her bottom, gently kneading her flesh with his fingers. He lifted her off her feet and she wrapped her legs around his hips as he carried her to the bed. With eager impatience, she lay watching as he pulled off his boots, then trousers and underpants. When he stood before her, his strength and virility painted silver by the glowing moonlight, she opened her arms and thighs to him, inviting his possession.

He moved over her, and the waiting passion between them exploded in consummate ecstasy. His name was torn from her lips as he claimed her.

Lesley stared up at the ceiling, watching the rays of the early morning sun consume the night shadows and fill the room with a golden glow. After a moment she turned her head to study the man lying at her side. The crescent sweep of his dark lashes lay motionless against the bronze curve of his cheeks, his breathing was deep and relaxed. Sleep had ironed the hard lines of his face, giving it a softer, more boyish cast. His mouth was relaxed in a faint smile, and she resisted the temptation to trace its outline with the tip of her finger.

Last night she had avoided conscious thought on how she might feel this morning. In the back of her mind though, she had expected guilt, regret perhaps, uncertainty as to where they went from here. She felt nothing like that.

An intense sense of *rightness* had swept through her when she'd awoken and found Zack at her side. Married, unmarried, divorced, none of those paper things mattered. He was her man, her mate in every way that mattered. Theirs was a bonding of the soul that transcended courts and record offices and ministers. She wondered how she could ever have imagined it could be any other way.

Still filled with the gentle langour that was the aftermath of last night's lovemaking, she edged towards him. Bending her head close to his, Lesley lightly ran her tongue over his full lower lip. She felt him stir and moved back to watch his grimace as he fought against consciousness. As his face relaxed once again, she repeated the manoeuvre, then teased the corners of his mouth with her lips as she ran her palms over his chest. This time when she moved her head back, though his eyes remained closed, she could tell from the set of his mouth that he was only feigning sleep.

She smiled to herself, and continued to let her fingers explore the mat of hair covering the hard wall of his chest. Encountering the rigid nub of a male nipple, she caressed it with her fingertip, then trailed her hand downward across his ribs to his hip. Allowing it to rest there in tantalising uncertainty, she watched his features. His eyelids twitched involuntarily, before he exercised rigid control to reinstate the masklike blandness of false sleep.

Lesley sighed gustily and abruptly turned away to present him with her back. Stifling a giggle, she sensed his astonishment. Four heartbeats passed, and then his hand shot out to grasp her shoulder and he rolled her on to her back. Propping himself above her, Zack scowled down into her ingenuous blue eyes.

'You shouldn't start things you're not prepared to finish, my dear,' he growled.

'But I thought you were still asleep.' She fluttered her eyelids innocently.

'Did you, now?' He shifted closer until she could feel his awakened virility against her thigh. 'Does that feel as if I'm asleep?' His hands cupped her breasts, and he fondled the raspberry nodes of her nipples as he smiled down at her.

Lesley ran the tip of her tongue over her lips, and moved her hips in provocation. His mouth homed in on hers as his hand slid over her flat belly. The kiss deepening, his tongue probed the sweet moistness of her mouth as his fingers investigated that tender haven below. Blissful desire flooded through her and she arched towards him, a soft, primitive sound in her throat. Her arms embraced him, her hands caressing his back and buttocks in exploratory wonder.

Timeless moments of delight passed as they rediscovered the hidden secrets of one another's bodies, stroking, caressing, tasting. It was slow and easy love-play, a gradual ascent to passion, unrushed and unhurried. With heightening sensitivity, Lesley's nerve-ends tingled with awareness as anticipation of fulfilment built.

The harsh ring of the bedside phone shattered the heady atmosphere of erotica. Instantly, Lesley tensed, her fingers faltering in their exploration of Zack's ribcage.

He leaned his head to her ear, whispering, 'Relax. Ignore it.' Catching the lobe between his teeth, he gently tugged at it.

Lesley did not relax. 'It might be important.' Twisting her head away from his questing lips, she looked towards the clock. 'It's barely seven o'clock. Nobody would call at this hour on a weekend unless it was important. Something might have happened to Mandy.'

With a sense of rising panic, Lesley struggled free of Zack's confining limbs and rolled to the side of the bed. Zack gave her a look of burning frustration and subsided on to his back, his head resting on his pillow as he stared at the ceiling in disgruntled silence.

Swinging her feet over the side of the bed, Lesley snatched the receiver from its cradle and said into it, 'Hello?'

'Good morning. I'm sorry to disturb you, but I'd like to speak to Zack Mackenzie please.'

Lesley gulped. It wasn't Tina's parents, or a forest ranger, or a policeman, or any of the messengers of ill tidings she'd imagined. She supposed she should be thankful for that, but the woman's soft, melodious voice plunged her into a new kind of panic. Mandy had told her about the lady on the phone who called early in the morning. She called—and Zack went running to her.

'Are you still there?' she asked into Lesley's ear.

'Oh . . . oh, yes,' she forced the words past her tightened throat. Why hadn't she listened to Zack, and ignored the ringing phone? She wanted to throw the receiver back on to the hook and pretend she had never heard that voice.

'Well, could you get Zack for me if he's available? You can tell him it's Lisa calling.'

Lisa—a sweet, feminine name to go with the voice. A fierce anger unlike any she had ever imagined swept through her. Zack wasn't available —he was in her bed and unavailable to any other woman. How dared she call him here?

Her knuckles whitened as she gripped the phone. Glancing over her shoulder to Zack, she saw him smile. 'Who is it? Get rid of them and come back to bed.' He patted the space beside him intimately.

His action redirected her anger toward him, jealousy running through her like molten metal. Leaping to her feet, Lesley held out the phone to him. He frowned slightly on seeing her rage-pale face, and eased himself into a sitting position. She threw the receiver at him. 'It's for you . . . Lisa.'

As she swung around, he caught her wrist in a lightning movement, holding her back. 'Wait a minute, Lesley.'

Blue eyes blazing, she slashed him a look, and slapped his hand away. Rushing to grab her robe, she flung furious advice at him. 'Don't keep her waiting, Zack!'

He untangled the receiver from the bedclothes as she shrugged on her robe. Placing his hand over the mouthpiece, he commanded impatiently, 'Lesley! Wait!'

She cinched the belt of her robe tight and glared at him. 'No, thanks! Unlike *you* I don't get my kicks from listening in on other people's phone conversations.'

Turning on her heel, she stormed from the room.

*   *   *

Downstairs in the kitchen, Lesley stopped her head long flight and sagged against the door. She was trembling in the aftermath of intense emotion. Unconsciously, her eyes sought the wall phone, riveted to it with burning intensity. Despite what she had said about not wanting to eavesdrop, the desire to walk over to it and take up the receiver filled her.

She took a step towards it, then halted, self-loathing taking over from the anger and jealousy that had filled her. Staring down at her shaking hands, she muttered. 'What's got into me?' If Mandy had behaved as she had up in the bedroom a moment ago, she would have been grounded for a month. Mandy wouldn't have acted that way, though—she was too adult.

Running a distracted hand through her tumble of blonde hair, she tossed the phone one last look before walking to the counter to pick up the percolator. As she made the coffee, she asked herself again what was happening to her. Jealousy had never been one of her vices. When they had been married and Zack was on the road for weeks at a time, the one thing she had never done was flail him with suspicions and accusations when he came back to her. Not that she hadn't known that there were a lot of tempatations for a lone male on the rodeo circuit—barrel-racers, the usual collection of 'groupies'. But she had trusted him.

Setting the coffee-pot on a burner, she turned the heat on under it and leaned back against the counter. She had always trusted Zack, so she had never been jealous or suspicious. She had had faith in his integrity, his commitment to keeping to their wedding vows

Lesley stared down at her hands, their fingers unadorned. That was it, wasn't it? Her wedding ring lay upstairs in her jewellery box, where it had lain for the past five years. She had dissolved those wedding vows—and Zack had no reason to be faithful to her now. She'd told herself this morning that what they had together, what he meant to her, needed no paper bond, no preacher's blessing. But in her heart she knew she needed that open avowal.

'Lesley?' Zack's voice, coming from the doorway, startled her and she looked up at him. His expression was unreadable and she swiftly dropped her eyes from his. He was wearing the same trousers that he'd had on the previous night, but no shirt. Only moments earlier, her fingers had explored the crisp, curling rug of hair that covered his lean, well-muscled chest.

She swallowed the hard lump that had formed in her throat. 'I'm making some coffee,' she offered, her voice husky. Quickly turning away, she opened a cupboard door and took out two cups. Behind her, she could hear Zack's footfalls as he moved farther into the room.

'Lesley . . . about upstairs . . .'

'Look, I'm sorry,' she interrupted hastily, though she couldn't bring herself to face him. 'I don't know what got into me. I mean . . . it's none of my business, is it?'

Silence filled the room, then she heard him move closer. A moment later, his hands came up to rest lightly on her shoulders. 'You were jealous,' he stated, not quite able to conceal the satisfaction in his voice.

Lesley bit her lip. After the performance she'd given him upstairs, she could hardly deny it.

When she didn't reply, he continued. 'You never used to be. I sometimes wondered why. Was it because you didn't think anyone else would want me, or because you just didn't care if they did?'

'I would have cared,' she admitted roughly. 'I just . . . never thought you would. I mean, we were married and I . . .' She felt the pressure as his fingers tightened their hold and said quickly, 'Can't we just drop it? I was in the wrong. I had no right to get uptight just because your girlfriend called you, and I'm sorry. It caught me off guard and it won't happen again. I don't know why I acted like that.'

His thumbs were tracing small, evocative circles over her shoulderblades. 'Maybe you still care?' he suggested.

Ignoring that, Lesley stepped away from him. 'I think the coffee's almost ready. Should I start breakfast?'

'Lisa's not my girlfriend,' Zack said, ignoring her question in turn. Lesley had been reaching for the coffee-pot and her hand froze briefly in mid-air. The tension within her snapped like an over-burdened rubber-band, leaving her weak with relief. Again she moved to grasp the handle of the pot, but as her fingers closed over it she didn't think she had the strength to pick it up.

'She's not my girlfriend.' Zack reiterated. 'As a matter of fact, she's my very much married secretary.'

Abandoning the coffee, Lesley swung around to face him. 'Your what?'

'My secretary.'

'But . . .' She shook her head in confusion. Why would Zack need a secretary? I thought you worked at Sheridan's?'

'I do.' He couldn't suppress a slightly bitter twist to his mouth as she continued to look puzzled. He said, 'I work there, but I also own it.'

'Own it?' Lesley parroted. 'But it's a big company. You mean, you own one of their franchises?'

'No, I own Sheridan's,' he stated deliberately. 'It's mine. I bought into it a few years ago, and when I retired from rodeoing, I bought the other shareholders out.'

Lesley stared at him dumfoundedly. After a minute, she walked on shaking legs to the kitchen table and sat down on a chair. She needed to sit down. She turned her head to him and looked searchingly into his face. He wasn't teasing.

'But I thought . . . and nobody told me . . .'

'I know what you thought, and you didn't want to hear.'

Lesley looked away from him, staring down at her hands as her fingers laced and relaced themselves. There had been a hard edge of bitterness to Zack's voice, and she knew it was justified. She'd had faith in his fidelity, but faith in him as a man who could do something with his life had been sadly lacking. She used to get furious with her father because he always referred to Zack as 'that rodeo bum' and yet, deep down, she had labelled him that in her own mind. She'd even scoffed at him that day in the café when he'd hinted then of his success. No wonder he'd taken so long to tell her.

She glanced over to him, wondering what she could possibly say to him now. He held her eyes with his. She'd hurt him by her lack of confidence in him, yet, seeing her stricken look, he could nurse the hurt no longer. Smiling at her, he asked gently, 'Would you like me to tell you about it now?'

His change of mood dispersed the brittle animosity that had built up between them. Lesley moistened her lips with the tip of her tongue and nodded.

Zack grinned back at her. In that case, why don't you get us a couple of cups of that coffee and I'll tell you how I got to be a business tycoon?'

CHAPTER ELEVEN

ON MONDAY afternoon, Lesley sat in the kitchen making a half-hearted attempt to read the newspaper. It was yesterday's paper, and somewhat wrinkled. She'd risen before Zack the previous day and, along with coffee and toast, had brought the Sunday paper upstairs so that they could spend a lazy morning in bed. The coffee had grown cold and the paper had got somewhat tattered because Zack had had other ideas for morning recreations.

As she attempted to read the headline stories, the nagging disquiet that interrupted her concentration had little to do with the President's new 'tough-guy' defence policy or the rash of murders that had occurred in Denver during the last few months. John Murray had stopped by earlier with some problem concerning the farm, and Zack had gone off with him to sort it out. It was her farm and it had been her place to deal with John, but Zack seemed to have taken over the role of head of the house.

That was the source of her disquiet. Not that she wouldn't have welcomed Zack into the position had circumstances been otherwise. Without her even quite realising it was happening, she'd gradually grown to rely on him to keep the wheels of her life turning over during these past weeks. This weekend's sharing his bed was merely a culmination of the intimacy that had been growing between them. And she knew now that she wanted him back

151

in her life, she wanted to be his wife again.

Since his confession on Saturday of his real position at Sheridan's, though, she understood why he hadn't said anything about getting married again. It was one thing for a man in his position to have an affair with her, but you could hardly expect the head of a company like Sheridan's to saddle himself with a highschool drop-out waitress for a wife, even if he had once been married to her. He knew important people now, mingled with the upper stratum of society. He needed a wife who could fit into that world, and a farm girl from the sticks wasn't a likely candidate.

Abandoning the front-page headlines, Lesley leafed through the paper, not really seeing the printed words. How could she allow the present arrangement to continue after Mandy's return tonight? She didn't feel guilty about this weekend, but, if she allowed it to go on with her child's knowledge, she didn't think that she could look her daughter in the eye ever again. Maybe she was a hypocrite, but she promoted the old-fashioned morality of virginity and white weddings to her daughter. Most of the time, she thought she set a good example for her. Carrying on an affair right under the child's nose was hardly that, though, even if the man was her ex-husband.

Which meant that somehow she was going to have to eject Zack from her bed. She didn't want to argue with him, she didn't want a rift, but she knew Zack well enough to know he wasn't going to meekly move back into his camper tonight.

She'd been staring blankly at the printed news-sheet for several minutes trying to find the right words to tell him that that was exactly what he was going to have to do, when his name jumped out at her. She glanced to the top of the page and saw that she had stumbled into the sport section. The article with his name in it was a special feature on rodeoing.

Shelving her problem, she started to read. She had to admit to a surge of pride as she skimmed through the glowing account of Zack's achievements on the rodeo circuit, and his later successes in the world of business. Suddenly though, her eyes faltered, riveted to the words the sports writer had penned.

. . . Although he is now retired, rodeo fans will have one last opportunity to see Zack Mackenzie in action. With proceeds going to the PRA Special Fund, he, along with other former rodeo greats, will perform in an exhibition afternoon at this year's Cheyenne Stampede. Of special interest is that Mackenzie will be riding Cherry Bomb, the bull that ended his rodeo career two years ago when he fell, severely injuring . . .

Lesley couldn't read any further, her mind filling with the image of a day long ago. It had been one of the rare times she'd left Mandy with her parents while she'd gone on the road with Zack. Mandy had been almost five then, and Lesley saw her trip as a last-ditch attempt to save her marriage. They couldn't go on as they had been doing for ever. If this time she couldn't get Zack to quit the rodeos, well, then, maybe she would be the one who would have to give in.

There'd been a cold wind sweeping down from the Rockies over the rodeo grounds that day. Its chill touched her even now. She and Besty had been standing together by the fence next to the bucking chutes, and Zack had already completed his ride for the day. He'd looked disgusted when he'd bailed off the bull when the bell had sounded after eight seconds. A rider was judged not only on his performance, but that of the bull's as well. Zack's bull had done poorly, running instead of bucking for most of the time, and the resulting score had placed him way out of the money.

Jerry was riding next. The chute gate had swung open, and Betsy's husband had come out on a piebald fury. It had twisted almost tail to nose on that first buck out of the chute, but Jerry had tenaciously hung on to the rope tied around its belly. Gyrating and bellowing, the animal frantically tried to unseat the enemy on its back. A breathless hush settled over the crowd as the battle raged, then Jerry's hand had slipped, and he'd gone flying through the air . . .

'John and I had to run into Longmont to get some parts, so I picked up some steaks for supper tonight while we were there,' Zack said from behind her. Lesley started, coming back to the present abruptly. She hadn't heard the pick-up returning or Zack entering the house. She looked over to him as he walked to the counter to deposit the bag he was carrying, then back at the newspaper spread out in front of her.

Zack started unpacking the groceries, whistling tunelessly to himself. After a moment, he noticed Lesley's silence and turned to look at her. 'What's the matter?' he asked abruptly, seeing her expression.

Lesley gave him a hard look. All the warnings her parents had given her, the fear they had nurtured, had come flooding back to her, and anger that he could do such a thing overwhelmed her. Grabbing the paper, she thrust it towards him.

Taking it from her, he glanced down at it. After reading the section heading, he looked back at her with a puzzled air.

'Just read it, Zack.'

He shrugged, and moved his eyes down the column of print. She knew the moment he reached the part about his riding in Cheyenne, because his jaw firmed and his expression took on an obstinate cast. It was still there when he looked up, tossing the paperback on to the table in front of her.

'Well?' Lesley demanded, when he didn't seem to be going to explain.

'Well, what?' Zack came back. 'They got my name right. Pretty flattering article, although I think the fellow overdid the flowery adjectives.'

'I wasn't asking for a critique of the guy's writing style, and you know it. Are you going to be riding at Cheyenne?'

He held her eyes, his emitting a warning. 'Yes, I am,' he admitted quietly.

She stared back him, unconsciously shaking her head. There had been a faint hope that there had been a mistake, that the reporter had got his facts mixed. It died an unnatural death with his words.

'No!' she cried. 'You can't. How could you? You quit the rodeo, you don't ride the bulls any more. You can't!'

'I can and I will,' Zack said with deliberation.

'But why? You don't have to. You're a business-man now, you told me so. You don't need to do it.'

'But I do need to,' he replied. He lowered his head, rubbing the back of his head distractedly before looking back at her. 'Try to understand. I *have* retired from the rodeos and I'm not going back on the circuit. But I have to make this one last ride. I have to prove to myself that I can do it. I may never get another chance. When I quit . . . . it wasn't the way I wanted to go out. It's nagged me ever since. Did I really quit because I couldn't calf-rope any more, or was it that I had just lost my nerve? This opportunity came along and . . .' He shrugged.

'That's it?' Lesley asked appalled. 'Ego . . . that's why you're doing it? Risking you life just to prove you're some kind of macho man? Have you forgotten what happened to Jerry . . . my God, have you forgotten that a bull crippled you?'

His eyes were flint hard as he met hers. 'I haven't forgotten, but I have to do it anyway. Maybe it is just some kind of an ego trip, but my self-image requires that I don't back out now.'

'I'm not going to let you do this!' she cried, jumping up from her chair to confront him with blue eyes flaming.

If possible, his face grew colder. 'You can't stop me. Maybe that's been our problem all along. You never were content to let me just be me, to make my own decisions. You always wanted to dictate to me, tell me how to run my life. Well, look, lady, you're not my wife any more, and even if you were, I still wouldn't let you put me on a leash and lead me around like some tame dog. You'd better look elsewhere if that's what you want in a man.'

'I want someone who gives a little care and attention to *my* feelings and needs, and not some selfish bastard bent on killing himself,' Lesley retorted. 'And I guess I will have to look elsewhere. In the meantime, I've asked you to leave I don't know how many times, but you haven't. This time, would you just clear out?'

'Fine.' He paused, the tension hanging between them like an electric field. After a moment he folded his arms in front of his chest, giving her an assessing look. 'Before I go, though, I'll give you a bit of advice. If you're looking in the direction of your friend Brian, look again. He's welcome to you, but I won't let him have Mandy. I'll want custody of her.'

Lesley reached out and grasped the back of the chair she had been sitting in. There was no logical reason to fear Zack's words. He had no grounds for taking Mandy from her, even if she did marry Brian. None the less, her knuckles turned white under the pressure of her grip. 'What are you threatening me with?'

'I'm not threatening, I'm telling you. Go ahead and marry this Brian fellow if you want to, but he's not going to be stepfather to my daughter. You'll have a fight on your hands. I know all about stepfathers—I'll not let my daughter go through that!'

Some of the tension eased out of her. 'I know what you're getting at, but you're wrong. Brian's nothing like the man your mother married. He and Mandy get along wonderfully. She adores him.'

'That's not the impression she gave me.'

'Well, it's the truth,' Lesley said flatly. 'I don't know what tales she's been telling you, but Brian's been more of a father to her than you ever have. She'd be lucky to have him for her stepfather.'

Before Zack could respond, Mandy rushed to her father from the doorway. 'No! No!' she shouted. 'I don't want Brian, I don't want Mom to marry him. I want my real father!' Her arms wrapped around

Zack's waist in a desperate hold, she turned her head and stared accusingly at Lesley. 'Why won't you marry Daddy, if you want to marry somebody? Brian's my friend, but I don't want him to be my father!'

Appalled, Lesley looked back at her daughter. How long had she been standing in the doorway listening to them argue? She hadn't heard the car dropping her off, she hadn't heard anything but the furious exchange between her and Zack. 'Mandy . . .' she said helplessly, shaking her head.

'I hate you!' the child screamed at her. 'I hate you! I heard you telling Daddy he had to leave. I want to go with him. He said he wanted custa-custa-what-ever-it-was, and I want you to give it to him. I want my Daddy!'

Lesley's eyes were a dark, bruised blue in her chalk-white face. She felt lacerated by her daughter's words, as though she were bleeding to death. Nausea filling her, she lowered her head, biting her lip until the salty blood taste filled her mouth.

After an interminable silence, she heard Zack say, 'You can't go with me, Mandy, but I am leaving. When you're older, if you still want to come live with me you can. For now, though, the law says that you have to stay with your mother.'

'Well, make the law change,' Mandy argued.

'I can't do that,' Zack said gently. Lesley glanced quickly over to him. There was still hostility in his gaze, but mingling with it was pity as well. She'd accused him of not caring for her feelings, but knew she had been unjust. Their differences lay between them like a gaping chasm, unbridgable and unassailable. However, he wouldn't take her child from her. Tears flooded her eyes and she averted her face. He was taking himself, though, and she knew he'd never come back.

Zack said, 'I have to leave now, Sweet-knees. You behave yourself and look after Sugar. She'll probably be lonely for a while without Clancy, so you be extra nice to her.'

With his arm around his daughter's shoulders, he led her from the kitchen. As the outside door closed behind, Lesley could no longer contain the sobs welling within her throat.

Over the next few weeks, Lesley suffered through the hot, dry Colorado summer, coping with a loneliness of spirit that was new to her. There was a sharp ache in her heart whenever she thought of Zack—and she thought of him often. At night, lying sleepless in the big double bed they'd shared, she was filled with a vast emptiness, as empty as the space beside her. After their divorce, she had not felt so shattered, although lord knew that had hurt enough. She'd had her parents, though, and Mandy . . .

Since the afternoon of Zack's departure there had been a barrier between her and her daughter that she couldn't seem to breach. When school ended for the long break, Lesley had hoped that they would naturally fall into the habits of companionship and friendship that had marked other summers, but she was disappointed. Every day, Mandy rose early and rode off alone on Sugar, roaming over the farm and the nearby countryside and avoiding her mother.

Although she'd been hurt by Mandy's avowal of hate, Lesley had been a mother long enough to know that children often made impassioned statements that they didn't really mean. However, as the weeks passed and their relationship deteriorated, Lesley couldn't help but wonder if maybe her daughter really did hate her for sending Zack away.

Given the atmosphere between them, when Brian returned to Colorado and called to suggest an outing, Lésley had put him off. Just now Mandy seemed such a stranger that Lesley didn't know how she'd react to seeing Brian. She didn't want him hurt by encountering open hostility from the girl.

Towards the end of June, Betsy dropped in for a visit. Lesley was in the house when she arrived, and when she looked out and saw the other woman, her first thought was that Zack must have sent her to pick up Mandy for a visit with him. Consequently, Lesley went out to meet her friend with very mixed feelings. On the one hand, it would almost be a relief to have a break from the strain of her antagonistic daughter's presence for a while. However, things might be even worse between them after Mandy came back from seeing her father.

Mandy had heard the car as well, and had come from the barn to join Betsy by the time Lesley walked out of the house. As she approached the pair, Lesley watched the young girl. She was bubbling over with animation, giggling at some remark of Betsy's, her face split wide with a grin. It seemed like years since she'd seen her daughter smile, and a smile softened her own features.

When she reached the two standing by Betsy's car, though, Mandy's high spirits vanished and she shot her mother a look of resentment. Lesley's smile faltered under the girl's enmity, but she managed to re-establish it as she greeted her friend.

'I hope you'll stay for supper,' Lesley said once the salutations were out of the way.

'Longer than that, I hope, if you'll put up with me,' Betsy replied, surreptitiously studying Lesley's strained features, then sliding a quick glance at Mandy's sullen ones. She continued. 'Matt's down in Texas and I didn't feel like going with him, so I thought maybe I'd bum a bed off of you for a few days if that's OK.'

'That would be great. You're always welcome here.' Although she made her tone hearty, Lesley's blue eyes held faint concern as she met the other woman's. Had things already started to go wrong for Betsy and Matt?

The other woman picked up on Lesley's qualms. Leaving them unspoken, she assured her, 'I thought I'd take things easy for a while—that's why I didn't go with Matt.' She held up crossed fingers. 'I'm hoping that I've started a baby, and Matt doesn't want me taking any chances with it.'

'Betsy, how wonderful!' Impulsively, Lesley hugged her friend. During her marriage to Jerry, Betsy had longed to conceive a child. Unfortunately, Mother Nature hadn't co-operated, much to the other woman's disappointment. Lesley'd had a lot of doubts about Betsy's marriage to a rodeo man, but if Matt could give her a child, then maybe it was what was right for her friend.

Stepping back from her, Lesley gave her a pleased smile. 'Let's not stand out here in the hot sun. Come on inside and you can tell me all about it.' She started to link her arm through the other woman's, when Mandy interrupted.

'I want Betsy to see Sugar before she goes inside,' the child demanded, her tone bordering on rudeness. She stepped forward and caught Betsy's hand to lead her towards the barn.

Lesley gave her daughter a warning look, but held her temper. She wasn't going to let her provoke her into an argument in front of her old friend. 'Betsy's just had a long drive. We'll let her get settled first, then you can show her your horse. Why don't you bring her cases in and put them upstairs in Grandma and Grandpa's old room while I make us all some lemonade?'

'I want her to see the horse Daddy gave me now!' Mandy insisted, tugging at Betsy's hand. Her chin jutted out in defiance, her brown eyes shining with challenge. Lesley looked back at her in angry bewilderment. Mandy had always been such a tractable child. She had always respected Lesley's authority. Oh, they'd had their ups and downs, but by and large their relationship had been placid, based as it was on a solid footing of love and affection.

All that had changed in this past month, though. She knew Mandy was upset about her and Zack, and consequently had tried to ignore the child's sulks and insolence. It hadn't seemed the time to come down on her as the 'heavy' mother, exerting her authority and demanding her daughter's respect. As a result, Lesley had walked on eggshells trying to avoid an altercation. However, it was one thing to ignore her misbehaviour in private but quite another to put up with it in front of an audience.

Before Lesley could react, though, Betsy's voice broke into the tense atmosphere of antagonism. 'I'm just dying for a cold drink.' She gently disengaged her hand from Mandy's. 'Let your mom fix me one and then I'll come out to see your horse. In the meantime, you can bring my suitcase into the house so that I can open it up and get you your present.'

'What did you bring me?' Mandy asked eagerly.

Betsy handed her the car keys. 'The suitcase is in the trunk. Take it up to my room and you'll find out as soon as I get it unpacked.'

Mandy skipped around to the back of the car, avoiding her mother. The two woman watched as the girl pulled the case from the trunk of the car and started with it towards the house. After a moment, Lesley glanced over to find Betsy watching her. She felt her cheeks heat with embarrassment. Betsy had deftly defused the tense moment between her and her daughter and she was grateful to her. However, she wished her friend hadn't been witness to it in the first place.

'Let's go get that lemonade,' she suggested hastily. 'I could do with a drink myself.'

Betsy hesitated and Lesley looked away, hoping that she would accept the diversion. Maybe later, when Mandy was in bed and out of the way, she'd talk to her friend about her problems with her daughter . . . maybe even talk about Zack.

A sudden uprush of tears caught her unawares and she hastily blinked them back. Besty would want to talk babies, and Lesley knew that was going to hurt. She and Zack had been reckless that weekend and hadn't taken any precautions. However, there weren't going to be any repercussions. She knew it was stupid of her, but Lesley wished that there had been. Maybe a baby would have given her a way back to Zack. Even if it hadn't, it would have been another part of him to hold on to.

Sensing her friend's frail hold on her composure, Betsy didn't probe. 'I'm dying for that drink. I might even help you squeeze the lemons!' she offered. Tucking her arm in Lesley's, they walked to the house.

CHAPTER TWELVE

'I DON'T think that I had much choice but to ask him to leave,' Lesley said. 'I mean, what can you do with a man who seems bent on killing himself?' She was standing in the living-room by the window, staring out into the dark night. Behind her, Betsy was curled up on the sofa and had been listening to her pour out her troubles for the past hour. It was the last night of her friend's visit, and tomorrow she would be going back to Cheyenne to meet Matt who was coming back from Texas.

The five days that Betsy had been at the farm had flown, not dragged as the month previous to her arrival had. The other woman's presence had served as a buffer between herself and Mandy, and Lesley wasn't looking forward to her departure. Although this was the first opportunity that she had had to confide in her about Zack, just having her around had somehow eased the pain she was feeling over their estrangement.

Lesley turned back into the room and looked over to her now. 'I'm right, aren't I? Riding that bull is just some stupid ego thing with Zack.'

Betsy didn't look up at her but stared down at the carpeting, seeming to find something fascinating about the tweed shag. As Lesley waited for her to say something, she realised that her friend had said very little over the past hour. When it appeared that she wasn't intending to reply now, either, Lesley said sharply, 'I am right, aren't I?'

The other woman shrugged and Lesley made an impatient sound, causing her to look up. She said, 'If that's the way you feel, then there's not a lot I can say.'

'But you agree with me, don't you?' Lesley insisted. Ever since Zack had left, Lesley had been telling herself she'd done the right thing. It *must* have been the right thing to do.

Betsy's discomfort was obvious. She moved uneasily in her seat as she avoided Lesley's eyes. Finally though, she linked her fingers and, meeting her friend's gaze, said quietly, 'No, I don't. If you love Zack, then whether he rides that bull or not shouldn't make any difference. I'm sorry, but that's the way I see it.'

Lesley stared at her in anger. She needed vindication of her actions, and she wasn't getting it. She didn't want Betsy voicing aloud what that nagging little voice inside her had been telling her all along. Lesley argued. 'I just can't understand you. After Jerry, how could you side with Zack on this? It's senseless for those men to risk their lives for nothing.'

'It's not nothing to them. It's the way they were made, something about the challenge that they can't ignore,' Betsy explained. Her glance moved away from Lesley briefly, then came back. Her features held resolution. 'I'm not siding with Zack exactly, but I think you've sensed all these years that I've never agreed with the way you've acted towards him. You knew he was a rodeo man when you married him, but ever since then, you've tried to change him. You mentioned his ego—well, what about yours? How much of wanting him to quit had to do with the danger of his getting hurt and how much was just you wanting him to prove how he loved you by giving into you?'

'It's a dangerous sport,' Lesley protested.

'Then he needed all the support you could give him, didn't he?' He needs it *now*,' Betsy emphasised. 'If you really loved him you'd stick by him. You'd never have broken up your life together.' Seeing the flames of angry colour creeping up Lesley's cheeks, she held up her hand to hold her silent. 'I know I'm talking out of turn, but it had to be said. What if that bull in Cheyenne does kill him? Where's this attitude of self-righteousness going to get you then? Are you to stand over his grave and say, "I was right. I told you so"? Is that going to make you feel better? The hardest thing I've ever had to face in this life was seeing Jerry killed, but I loved him and he knew it to his last breath. That knowledge helped me to get through the lonely years afterwards.'

A heavy silence fell over the room when Betsy finished speaking. Lesley could hear her own heartbeat, and a tight band seemed to be wrapped about her chest, making it difficult for her to breathe. She felt as though she had been bludgeoned. Her anger with Betsy had receded, leaving a bleak knot of pain within her heart. Unable to face the other woman any longer, Lesley abruptly turned back to the window. Unconsciously gripping the edge of the curtain, she stared blankly at her blurred reflection in the pane. She didn't see it, but instead the image evoked by Betsy's words—Zack's grave. For all her protests against his riding the bulls, that image had never been so sharply etched within her mind.

That weekend together she'd seen his scars. The upper thigh of his crippled leg where the surgeons had attempted to repair the damage was networked with them. As she'd run her fingertips over them, she'd felt sad and angry and frustrated that he should carry such marks.

But it had been *living* flesh beneath her touch. Warm and vibrant and alive. What if he were killed? What if he never felt his heartbeat beneath her ear again as she cradled her in his arms? What if he went to his grave not knowing she loved him?

'I do love him,' Lesley whispered roughly.

'Then don't you think you ought to let him know it?' Betsy asked gently. 'Be there when he rides in Cheyenne. Don't let him get on that bull without knowing it.' She stood and walked over to the other woman. Lightly touching her shoulder in a conciliatory manner, she said, 'I'm sorry if I've offended you, but somebody had to say it. At least think about it.' Her hand fell to her side. 'I'd like to go up to bed now. Are you OK?'

Lesley nodded, then turned her head and gave Betsy a weak smile. 'You go on . . . you need your rest. I'm fine, so don't worry about me. I'll be heading that way myself in a few minutes.'

After bidding her goodnight, Betsy left the room, leaving Lesley to her contemplation of the darkened windowpane. Deep down, she knew her friend was right . . . she had to see Zack, to let him know that she loved him before he rode Cherry Bomb in Cheyenne.

It wasn't going to be easy, though. She *was* proud, she didn't climb down easily. However, if she really loved him, she knew she had to tell him so, had to accept him as he was. She should have done it years ago, instead of listening to her parents and her own stubborn ego.

But now, of course, he didn't love her any more, she realised, swallowing a hard lump in her throat. She had destroyed his love by cutting him out of her life. That weekend he'd shared her bed, there had been no avowals of love. He desired her, but that wasn't the same thing, and he didn't want to remarry her . . . if he had, he would have said something. Worriedly, she ran her hand through her hair, then nibbled the tip of her thumb. If she went to him . . . *when* she went to him, it would have to be on his terms.

Turning away from the window, she walked to the easychair and slumped into it. Mandy's picture on the top of the television stared back at her. It was an aspect of the situation that she had to deal with. She loved her daughter, she wanted what was best for her. But what was the best? Mandy missed her father. She wanted and needed more than just the odd weekends and holidays that Lesley had restricted their relationship to. This last month had shown Lesley that, if nothing else.

There was the sound of movement behind her, and Lesley turned her head. Her daughter was standing in the doorway, holding a glass of milk.

'I came down for a drink and I saw the light. I thought maybe Betsy was in here.' the girl said defensively.

'She's gone to bed,' Lesley explained, sighing faintly. Mandy's whole demeanour shouted that she would never have come in here if she'd known her mother was here alone. Before the girl could flee, Lesley asked, 'Couldn't you sleep? Did you have a nightmare?'

'I was just thirsty,' she said flatly. Suiting her

actions to her words, she drained the milk from the glass, then started to turn away.

'Wait a minute, Mandy,' Lesley stayed her. 'Can we talk for a minute?'

'I don't want to talk to you,' Mandy said with hostility, although she didn't leave the room.

That was something, anyway, Lesley thought bitterly, standing up so that she could face the child. At least she was in the same room for a moment.

'I wanted to talk about your dad,' she admitted, trying to ignore the child's aggressive stance.

'Well, if you're going to tell me what a rotten person he is or something, I won't listen to you!'

How had they come to this? Lesley wondered sadly. If she'd seldom spoken of Zack to Mandy, she'd never run him down to her either. She didn't agree with divorced parents who dragged their children into their private disputes and tried to divide their loyalties.

'It wasn't anything like that,' she assured her. 'Nothing like that at all.'

'Well, then, what do you want to say?' Mandy asked bluntly, her gaze challenging with defiance.

At that moment, Lesley realised she didn't really know what she should say. She dropped her eyes away from her child's and stared down at the floor. How could she build up her daughter's hopes before talking to Zack? He might not want her back in his life on *any* terms.

She looked back up to Mandy and saw her growing impatience with her silence. Any moment, she would walk out on her, Lesley knew, and said finally. 'I wondered what you'd think about going to see him ride in Cheyenne.'

For a tense moment, Mandy simply stared at her,

then her features slowly started to relax. 'Do you mean it, Mom?' she asked cautiously.

Lesley nodded, smiling as she saw her daughter's smile break through. The girl's next question rocked her though, wiping the smile from her face. 'Does that mean you're going to get back together and get married again?'

'Well . . .' Lesley moistened her lips. 'Maybe not exactly. It . . . depends on a lot of things,' she said inadequately.

Mandy looked thoughtful, then slowly nodded. 'Yes, I suppose you and Dad probably should just live together for a while first,' she advised with shocking sophistication.

Lesley gave her a disbelieving look. 'What did you say?'

Mandy looked steadily back at her with an air of worldly wisdom that sat oddly on her childish features. 'Oh, I know what you've said about some day the right man will come along and I'll get married to him and everything, but me and my friends have talked about it. How will we know it's not just a sex thing——' *a sex thing*! Lesley thought '—if we don't find out what it's like living with him first?' Her mother was too nonplussed to respond, so she continued, 'We figured it might be better to find out if we were com—compat . . .' she stumbled over the word. Automatically, Lesley supplied it. 'Compatible, that's it. Anyway, it might be better to find out whether he leaves his socks lying around all over the place, or gets toothpaste all over the bathroom and stuff, before we got married to him.'

'I see,' Lesley said faintly.

'So, Mom,' Mandy went on confidently wallowing in her advisory capacity, 'you and Dad really

ought to try it out first before you get married. I
know you were married before, but you've probably
forgotten what it was like. You wouldn't want to get
a divorce again because you found out that he snores
or something.'

'No, I don't suppose I would,' Lesley admitted.
Someone older than eleven must have been talking
to her, probably one of her friend's teenage sisters.
The words and phrases sounded as though she was
parroting something she had heard rather than
thought out for herself—*sex thing*, indeed! Lesley
supposed she should be outraged, but instead she
found she was battling with an unholy desire to
laugh—mainly at herself. She'd been tying herself in
knots worrying about the moral implications of
'living in sin' with Zack, and Mandy didn't even
seem aware of that aspect of the situation.

Maybe whoever had been talking to her wasn't so
wrong, either. 'Living in sin'—what an archaic
term! There was a lot more involved in a man-
woman relationship than sharing a bed, and it was
gratifying to know that her daughter seemed to
realise that. Yes, Mandy's advice was actually very
sensible, even if Lesley *hadn't* forgotten what being
married to Zack was like and already knew that he
didn't snore.

She gave the girl an affectionate glance, opening
her arms to her in invitation. As her arms encircled
her in a loving hug, she dropped a kiss on her
daughter's wise little head.

The area behind the chutes was in chaos. As Lesley
skirted the pens filled with milling animals to reach
the open area filled with horse-trailers and rodeo
contestants, her eyes roamed in search of Zack's

tall, lean figure. In the distance she could hear the rodeo announcer over the loudspeakers, the roar of the crowd as they applauded a rider. The afternoon programme was nearly finished, with only one event left before the bullriding.

Lesley still hadn't spoken with Zack. When she couldn't see him now, she felt a sudden intensification of the panic that had been growing in her since that morning.

Just about everything that could go wrong today had. Her resolve to talk to Zack, to find some path across that chasm of enmity that separated had grown over these past weeks. Several times she almost called him, almost got into her car to go in search of him. Somehow though it seemed better to wait until the day he was to ride at the Cheyenne Stampede before she confronted him.

She'd planned an early-morning start from the farm, expecting to reach Cheyenne before noon. Betsy had told her that Zack wasn't planning to go out to the rodeo arena until after lunch, since the bullriding event was last on the schedule. It would be late afternoon before Zack would ride. After dropping Mandy off with Betsy, Lesley would catch him at his apartment before he left.

It hadn't worked out that way. Her middle-aged Honda, never much to look at but always reliable, had spoiled its record and let her down that morning. After ten minutes of trying to get it started, she'd waylaid John going through her yard out to the fields and asked him for help.

He'd tinkered under the hood for more than hour, every few minutes calling out to her to try the ignition key again. Finally he'd come around to the driver's door, wiping his grease-covered hands with a rag as he told her the starter motor was broken. She could have wept, as though it had been a close friend who had died. It would take hours for him to fetch a replacement and install it.

In the end, John had taken her and Mandy over to Fort Lupton to a catch a bus into Greeley where they could transfer on to one going to Cheyenne. Of course, the schedules hadn't worked out. After stopping in every one-house town on the route, they'd reached the terminal in Greeley just as the Cheyenne bus was pulling out. During the wait for the next bus, Lesley had called Betsy to arrange for her to pick them up at the Cheyenne terminal and drive them out to the arena. Naturally, the traffic had been heavy and empty parking spaces almost non-existent.

Feeling faintly sick with anxiety, Lesley wondered if it might not be better for her to go and find Betsy and Mandy in the grandstand. She couldn't see Zack anywhere and he was down to ride in just a short time. How would she be able to make up twelve year's lack of support in a couple of rushed minutes, anyway?

Making one last visual survey of the area around the bull pens, Lesley turned to make her way back to the grandstand. She'd only taken a step when she saw him. He was leaning in the shade of a horse-trailer, talking with a young couple. Lesley stared at him, her heart aching. He looked devastatingly handsome as he tilted back his head to laugh at something one of his companions had said. His dark burgundy western shirt was open at the neck, his Stetson cowboy hat tipped back on his head. He wore buttery soft doe-skin chaps that hung low on his hips, and boots in the same peanut brown.

Lesley smoothed her damp palms down the side of her slacks before walking to him. She'd started out that morning, neat and clean in tailored blue slacks with a matching blouse of crisp cotton. Glancing down at herself, she saw her clothes now looked as though she'd just pulled them out of the laundry hamper. As she pushed her hair back from her face, she could feel the film of dust that covered it.

Her courage was ebbing fast. The young woman standing by Zack looked like she was a model who'd just stepped out the pages of an exclusive Western-wear catalogue. There was so little time, it might be better to wait until after his ride.

Lesley was hovering in uncertainty when he looked over and saw her. The white slash of his smile disappeared as his eyes bore into hers. They were hard, brown slate and held no welcome. Abruptly, he turned his back to her, refocusing his attention on his companions.

Taking a deep breath, Lesley walked over to him. 'Zack?'

'Well, I'd better be getting over to the chute,' he told the couple, refusing to acknowledge Lesley. He turned and started to walk away.

Lesley stumbled after him, finally catching up and tugging at his sleeve. 'Please, Zack, I have to talk to you.'

He didn't stop until they'd reached the side of the pen holding the Brahmas. He looked down at her, his face carved in stone. 'I've heard it all before, so why don't you just get out of here and leave me alone? I'm riding that bull this afternoon whether you like it or not.' Resting his arms along the top railing of the fence, he studied the bulls, his posture dismissing her.

'I didn't come here to try to stop you,' Lesley assured him, her eyes pleading. He ignored her. 'Please, Zack, this isn't easy for me. I . . . I came to say I was wrong—that I should never have tried to make you quit rodeoing. I realise now that you have to do what you feel is right for you, and I shouldn't interfere.' Somewhat desperately, she said, 'I . . . I love you.' Her words weren't anything like the beautiful, well-polished speech she had practised in her mind over and over during the past weeks, and she waited breathlessly for his response.

His gaze remained fixed on the animals milling about the pen. Most of them were standing about idly chewing their cud and looked as docile as milch-cows. Lesley knew that some of them were actually quite tame. For the most part it was only in the arena, a man on their back and a taut bucking band around their flanks, that they became dangerous. A couple of them now, though, had caught the tension of the rodeo scene and were pacing restlessly about, pausing now and then to rake the dusty ground with their forefeet.

Zack kept her waiting for an agonisingly long time. Finally, he asked, his voice harsh, 'What brought on this about-face?'

Lesley licked her lips, glancing over to the bulls. Her hands reached out to the top rail and gripped it in a white-knuckled hold. A big sorrel Brahma cross was jostling his companions, tossing his head, his lethal-looking horns gleaming in the sunlight. 'I had to come before you rode. I . . . I didn't want,' she took a breath, trying to maintain her composure, 'I didn't want anything to happen to you without you knowing that . . . that I love you.'

'So, you think I'm going to get myself killed?'

Zack jeered. 'Sheridan's must be the attraction. You left it a little late for me to change my will. Don't worry, though. Since everything goes to Mandy anyway, you'll still benefit. After all, you are her legal guardian.'

Every scrap of colour had fled from her face when she turned to look at him with stricken blue eyes. 'How can you talk like that?' she whispered brokenly. 'I don't want your money, and I think you know that. I love you.' His expression didn't soften, and Lesley stared up at him helplessly, a skim of tears clouding the sky blue of her eyes. 'Oh, what's the use?' she asked, swinging around and walking away from him along the fence.

The animals on the other side were bellowing, all of them trotting restlessly about now as they were separated for loading into the bucking chutes. Over the noise, Lesley listened for the sound of Zack coming after her, but there were no footfalls behind her.

She stumbled, unable to see her way through the mist of tears that were threatening to spill over. She paused to blink them away, grasping the fence and feeling it vibrate beneath her fingers as a beast on the other side of it jostled against it.

She knew she had to get a grip on herself before she rejoined Betsy and Mandy . . . and God, what was she going to tell Mandy?

'Lesley!'

It took a moment for Zack's shout to register, then she jerked her head around to see him running towards her. She stared at him in bewildered joy and took a step forward, then a loud crack sounded behind her. An instant later, she was thrust to the ground, pain shooting through her ankle then echoing in her head as her temple slammed against a rock. Blackness dropped over her like a dark curtain.

CHAPTER THIRTEEN

FRETFULLY, Lesley brushed her hand over the dark, earthy stain on her slacks. It didn't alter and she doubted that it would come out even when they were laundered. Her blouse was in even worse shape, not only soiled, but torn in a couple of places too. She should have asked Betsy to bring her some fresh clothes. However, she supposed that the taxi-driver who would drive her to her girlfriend's apartment wouldn't be too interested in how she was dressed.

Shifting slightly in her chair in response to the ache in her ankle, Lesley wondered how much longer he would be. She wanted to get out of here.

Since arriving at the hospital by ambulance several hours ago, she'd been poked and prodded, X-rayed and taped until she was sick of it. Then some fool had brought her to this room—a *private* room and she could guess what it cost—instead of back into the emergency ward. She wasn't going to be using it, though. Maybe she did feel a bit rough, with the Chinese gong installed in her head going off every few minutes, and a throbbing ankle. However, she'd manage to get through the night at Betsy and Matt's somehow.

The door to the room opened, and Lesley quickly looked around, expecting the taxi-driver. Instead, Zack walked in, hesitating as he saw her sitting in the chair.

'I thought you'd gone,' she said. She had avoided

thinking about him, if the truth were known. She'd been blissfully unconscious during most of the trip to the hospital, though she'd surfaced once long enough to realise that Zack was with her.

He was probably furious, although after surreptitiously eyeing him from under her lashes, Lesley saw that he must be trying to hide it. He didn't look angry. However, as he had been scheduled to ride only a few minutes after the accident had happened, he couldn't have come to the hospital without missing his chance. He had to be furious with her, she thought, looking down to study her hands with intensity.

'I went back to the grounds to find Betsy and Mandy and let them know what happened,' he explained.

He didn't sound angry, either, and Lesley breathed a little more easily. He must have got back in time. 'So you were able to make your ride, after all.' She wasn't sure whether she was relieved or not. She supposed she was, although she really hadn't wanted him to ride. He'd come through it safely, though. 'How did it go?'

'I didn't ride,' he said flatly.

'I'm sorry,' Lesley whispered. 'I . . . er . . .'

Zack interrupted, ignoring her apology. 'What are you doing dressed and out of bed? The doctor told me earlier that he'd be keeping you in for a couple of days.' He walked over to where she was sitting and looked down at her sternly.

'I'm not staying here.' Lesley gestured to the room with its functional hospital bed and utilitarian furnishings. At least they were off the topic of his riding. 'This may not look like much, but I'll bet it costs more to stay here one night than it does for a whole week at the Hilton. Betsy won't mind putting me up for the night.'

'I'm paying for it, so you might as well stay here.'

Lesley shot him a quick glance and saw the hard set of his features. She looked down again at her hands resting in her lap. She wished her head would stop aching. She wasn't up to a big argument. None the less, she said, 'I can't let you do that.'

'Why not? You're my wife.'

She swallowed. 'That's just it, I'm not. I'm your *ex*-wife.' She raised her head to meet his eyes, her determination matching his. 'I won't take charity. You ought to know me well enough to know that.' She saw he was about to say something and got in first. 'Your responsibilities to me ended with the divorce.'

He met her statement with heavy silence and Lesley dropped her eyes again, nervously outlining the stain on her slacks with her fingertip. She started slightly when Zack laid his hand on her shoulder.

'You're wrong, Lesley,' he said softly. 'For a long time I thought that was what the divorce meant, too, but it didn't.' His fingers gently explored the bones of her shoulder, kneading her flesh, then sliding beneath the heavy fall of her hair to stroke her nape. Unconsciously, Lesley responded to him, flexing her muscles of her neck in supplication.

Moving, Zack knelt in front of her, clasping her hands in his. As he looked down at them, he rubbed the finger where his ring had lain between his thumb and forefinger. 'You're still my wife,' he said. 'The ring's gone, but the feeling never has. We're still married in our hearts.' He looked up and captured her eyes, holding them in a steadfast gaze. 'When

I brought out Sugar for Mandy, that wasn't the only reason I came. You know now that I didn't need a place to stay. When you jumped to that conclusion, though, I let you go on thinking it so you'd let me stay. You see, I was afraid you might be thinking of marrying this Brian fellow. I thought it bothered me because I wasn't sure of the kind of stepfather he'd make for Mandy.'

'Oh.' Lesley's thoughts were a jumble, but the warmth of his hands holding hers was spreading to her. She didn't understand exactly why Zack had changed. He'd sent her away that afternoon, but now he was here—holding her, caring for her, talking to her in soft, gentle tones.

'You didn't want me to marry Brian because of Mandy?' she roused herself to ask.

He smiled. 'That was only a small side issue. I soon discovered it was because of you. You're my wife . . . I couldn't let you be Brian's. I still can't.' His smile disappeared and he looked suddenly harsh. 'Have you seen him since I left the farm?'

'No,' Lesley assured him quickly. Zack's fingers had tightened on hers, and they slowly eased their hold as he heard her answer. 'He got back from Arizona, but I only talked to him on the phone. He wanted to get together, but I didn't go out with him. All he's ever been is just a friend, somebody to date, do things with. I liked him, I still do. He really did get along well with Mandy, and I suppose that's mostly why I saw so much of him.'

'You're not going to see him again, though,' Zack dictated sternly. He got to his feet and, lifting her from the chair, took her place then carefully set her in his lap. As his arms enfolded her, he asked sombrely, 'I'm not hurting you, am I?' Lesley shook her head. Zack's embrace had a mystic quality and, although she was still aware of her injuries, the pain was minimal. Even if she had been in agony, though, she wouldn't have wanted him to release her—ever.

'From the moment I came out of the barn with Mandy and saw you again, I knew my feelings hadn't changed,' Zack admitted. 'I still loved you, wanted you, felt you were mine.'

'But you sent me away today.'

His arms tightened around her. 'I know. I was a damn fool. I was hurt by your rejection of me and wanted to hurt you back.' His hands came up to cup her face, his eyes holding her. 'I was a damn fool. When I saw that bull going for you. I . . .' He shook his head, and Lesley felt the shudder that moved through him.

'I'm not that hurt, Zack,' she assured him. 'I'm just a little banged up.'

His gaze held doubt, and she leaned forward to brush his lips with her own. 'I'm all right now. I think I'll always be all right as long as I know you love me, because I love you so much. I never stopped loving you.'

Zack's embrace tightened as he drew her mouth to his, savouring the taste of love on her lips. After a long moment he eased her away, noting the stars he'd placed in her eyes. She clung to him, seeking to renew the kiss, but he held her firmly away. His smile mocked.

'You didn't act like it when I first showed up at the farm,' he said drily. 'You kept asking me to leave, if I recollect.'

'I know,' Lesley admitted sheepishly. 'You scared me. I was the one who had insisted on the divorce. I didn't want to admit even to myself that I'd made a mistake.' She bit her lip as a thought entered her head. 'I'm sorry you didn't get to ride this afternoon. It's my fault. I knew it meant a lot to you and I'm sorry . . .' she trailed off inadequately, keeping her head lowered.

'It doesn't matter.' He slipped his fingers under her chin and raised her face to look into it. 'It really doesn't matter,' he reiterated seriously. 'That part of my life is over, and the only regret I have is that I was too stubborn to end it sooner. I knew soon after we married that you hated the rodeo life, especially my riding the bulls. I've got a streak of obstinacy in me, though, and I guess the more you tried to get me to quit, the more I was determined to continue.' His eyes took on a rueful haze. 'God, I used to be so lonely on the road when you weren't with me. I hated that part of it, but kept on because I didn't want to give in to you.'

'I shouldn't have tried to make you.' Lesley snuggled closer to him, resting her head in the hollow beneath his shoulder. Her hands cradled his, running her fingers over the calloused skin of his palms. He was a tough, outdoors man, a cowboy, and she loved him as he was. She had been a fool to try to make him into something else. 'You loved the rodeos, the challenge . . . I should never have tried to force you to give it up.'

He hesitated. 'I don't want to make you angry, darling, but I think your parents had a lot to do with the way things were. I shouldn't have let you go to them after Mandy was born. I knew how they felt about me, and should have realised they would try to turn you against me.'

'I suppose you're right,' Lesley conceded sadly. She'd loved her parents very much, and now that they were dead and unable to defend themselves it seemed disloyal to admit their faults. Yet Zack was right. 'They did have a lot of influence on my actions. They were so good to me and Mandy, and I felt grateful to them. I should have stood up to them when they didn't want me to go back to you, but they played on my fear for you. They were always telling me how you were going to get yourself killed. I shouldn't have listened to them. I should have listened to my heart. I shouldn't have tried to change you, because then you wouldn't have been the man I fell in love with . . . that I still love.'

Placing his hand behind her neck, he held her head as his lips brushed over her in a light kiss. She made a little sound of protest as he edged her off his lap and got to his feet.

'No, Mrs Mackenzie, we're going to have to wait for a while. That bull did enough damage to you today, without my adding to it.' He dropped a brief kiss on her forehead and pushed her towards the adjoining bathroom. 'Now, why don't you get out of those clothes and into bed? Betsy gave me a nightie and some stuff for you to use when I stopped by her apartment on the way over. I left the suitcase out in the hall. I'll fetch it for you while you get undressed.' He started to turn away.

'I don't need to stay here in the hospital,' Lesley protested. 'I'm perfectly all right now.' In her agitation, she shifted her weight on to her injured ankle and gasped as pain shot up her leg.

Zack turned back in time to note her reaction. His smile chastised. 'Fit as a fiddle, are you? I'll get the suitcase.' His kiss stifled the protest hovering on her lips. Her resistance had turned to jelly by the time he lifted his head. He said, 'Promise me you'll stay in here until the doctor says you can leave, and not argue? It will be bad enough having a gimpy bridegroom at our wedding, without having to have the bride carried in on a stretcher.'

His hands dropped away and he'd moved to leave before Lesley managed to croak, 'Our wedding?'

Zack turned back. 'Of course, in a couple of weeks you ought to be ready for it.'

'But,' Lesley stopped to moisten her lips, staring at him uncertainly. 'you mean, you want to get married again?'

'Well, of course,' he assured her. 'That's what we've been talking about, isn't it?' His forehead creased as he frowned slightly. 'I guess I never actually made a formal proposal. I'd planned that for that evening when Mandy was supposed to come home from her camping trip, but . . .' He shrugged.

'Oh.' There had been a bottle of champagne in with the groceries Zack had brought in that afternoon. She'd wondered about it, but had dismissed it as being of no significance. Now she understood—he'd bought it to toast their engagement. 'I thought . . . I . . .'

'What did you think?'

She couldn't meet his eyes, and stared down at the floor. She murmured. 'I just thought you wanted me to be your mistress.'

'My mistress!' Zack exclaimed, an edge of temper in his voice. It set off Lesley's headache again. 'Whatever made you think that's all I wanted? I told you that I love you, that I feel that you're my wife. What were you thinking of? That we'd just live together? Is that what you were expecting when you came to me this afternoon? That we'd shack up? What about Mandy?'

Lesley trembled beneath the onslaught of his anger. Realising his temper had got out of hand, Zack swore softly under his breath and went to her. Slipping his arms around her waist, he held her to him.

'I'm sorry, Zack,' Lesley mumbled, loving the warm feel of his chest against her cheek. 'I . . . didn't want, I mean, I wanted us to get married, but I didn't think you did. All that weekend . . . you never said anything about it. Your life is a lot different now from when we first got married. You're a wealthy man.'

Zack's hand stroked the silken strands of her blonde hair. 'My money has nothing to do with anything.' he stated, so emphatically she had to believe him. 'It certainly hasn't changed the way I feel about you. As for that weekend . . . I didn't ask you then because of our argument the night I brought Mandy back from her horse meeting. I was sore because you wouldn't sleep with me, and was punishing you a little bit by keeping you hanging. When it got close to time for Mandy to come home, though, I knew I couldn't countenance our having that kind of dubious relationship with her around. I was going to ask you to marry me the night before she got back. Afterwards, I figured I'd move back out into my camper until we could make things legal.'

Lesley peered up at him. 'You would have?'

He grimaced. 'I wasn't looking forward to it, mind you. We are going to get married again, aren't we?'

An imp of mischief tugged at Lesley's sense of humour. She told him what Mandy had said about the advisability of living together before marriage. However, when she glanced up, she saw from

Zack's expression that he didn't find his daughter's advice either sage or humorous.

'That settles it. We're getting married just as soon as you get out of here. That young lady needs a full-time father to set her straight. If she thinks I'll stand by and watch her move in with her boyfriend some day, she can think again.'

'But, Zack,' Lesley protested, suddenly seeing Zack as the stern, Victorian father. 'this is the twentieth century! Why even you and I——'

'That was different,' Zack interrupted. 'You weren't my daughter.'

Lesley gave him an affronted look, then suddenly laughed. 'I'm awfully glad,' she bubbled, pressing closer to him.

He remained unresponsive for only a moment, then his laughter joined hers. 'So am I,' he whispered as his lips found hers.

Coming Next Month

#1215 FRIEND OR FOE Jenny Arden
Kira's late husband had given Glenn Mason guardianship over her stepdaughter, Heather—a fact Kira deeply resents. But his responsibility certainly doesn't give Glenn any right to interfere in her life—and sparks fly when he tries!

#1216 LOVERS TOUCH Penny Jordan
The only way Eleanor de Tressail can keep her promise to her grandfather to keep the estate in the family is a marriage of convenience to wealthy Joss Wycliffe. Only, for Eleanor, it is a case of love.

#1217 NOT WITHOUT LOVE Roberta Leigh
Julia's assignment is a challenge—to guard an engineer-inventor who has received death threats. Since Rees Denton refuses to have a bodyguard, Julia has to operate undercover as his personal assistant. But how can she watch over him at night?

#1218 WILD JUSTICE Joanna Mansell
Cassandra has enough problems coping with her overly possessive father, so she is furious when Jared Sinclair lures her to his isolated Scottish home for reasons entirely different from those he's given her. Surely it can't be just for revenge?

#1219 CHERISH THE FLAME Sandra Marton
Everyone's happy about Paige's forthcoming marriage to Alan Fowler—except his older brother, Quinn, who returns on the eve of the wedding. He tells Paige her father has been embezzling money from the Fowlers for years—and shocks her with the price for his silence!

#1220 THE DEVIL'S SHADOW Sally Wentworth
Her glamorous sister, Verity, spoiled Charlotte's early romance with Craig Bishop. Now, six years later, with Charlotte's dreams about to come true, Verity seems ready to do it again!

#1221 THE GATHERING DARKNESS Patricia Wilson
Nurse Julia Redford agrees to accompany her young patient Justine to her guardian's home in the Camargue. Julia has managed to cope with arrogant, overbearing Luc Marchal on her home ground, but once in France, Justine seems fine—and it's Luc who gives Julia problems!

#1222 BRAZILIAN FIRE Karen van der Zee
Chantal finds the sudden switch of life-styles from small-town America to the glamorous sophistication of Rio more than bewildering. She is even more puzzled by the cool, arrogant Enrico Chamberlain, who seems to hold her in such contempt!

Available in November wherever paperback books are sold, or through Harlequin Reader Service:

In the U.S.
901 Fuhrmann Blvd.
P.O. Box 1397
Buffalo, N.Y. 14240-1397

In Canada
P.O. Box 603
Fort Erie, Ontario
L2A 5X3

Especially for you, Christmas from
HARLEQUIN HISTORICALS

An enchanting collection of three Christmas
stories by some of your favorite authors captures
the spirit of the season in the 1800s

TUMBLEWEED CHRISTMAS by Kristin James

A "Bah, humbug" Texas rancher meets his match in his
new housekeeper, a woman determined to bring the spirit
of a Tumbleweed Christmas into his life—and love into
his heart.

A CINDERELLA CHRISTMAS by Lucy Elliot

The perfect granddaughter, sister and aunt, Mary Hillyer
seemed destined for spinsterhood until Jack Gates arrived
to discover a woman with dreams and passions that were
meant to be shared during a Cinderella Christmas.

HOME FOR CHRISTMAS
by Heather Graham Pozzessere

The magic of the season brings peace Home For
Christmas when a Yankee captain and a Southern heiress
fall in love during the Civil War.

Look for HARLEQUIN HISTORICALS CHRISTMAS
STORIES in November wherever Harlequin books are sold.

INDULGE A LITTLE SWEEPSTAKES

OFFICIAL RULES

SWEEPSTAKES RULES AND REGULATIONS. NO PURCHASE NECESSARY.

1. NO PURCHASE NECESSARY. To enter complete the official entry form and return with the invoice in the envelope provided. Or you may enter by printing your name, complete address and your daytime phone number on a 3 x 5 piece of paper. Include with your entry the hand printed words "Indulge A Little Sweepstakes." Mail your entry to: Indulge A Little Sweepstakes, P.O. Box 1397, Buffalo, NY 14269-1397. No mechanically reproduced entries accepted. Not responsible for late, lost, misdirected mail, or printing errors.

2. Three winners, one per month (Sept. 30, 1989, October 31, 1989 and November 30, 1989), will be selected in random drawings. All entries received prior to the drawing date will be eligible for that month's prize. This sweepstakes is under the supervision of MARDEN-KANE, INC. an independent judging organization whose decisions are final and binding. Winners will be notified by telephone and may be required to execute an affidavit of eligibility and release which must be returned within 14 days, or an alternate winner will be selected.

3. Prizes: 1st Grand Prize (1) a trip for two to Disneyworld in Orlando, Florida. Trip includes round trip air transportation, hotel accommodations for seven days and six nights, plus up to $700 expense money (ARV $3,500). 2nd Grand Prize (1) a seven-night Chandris Caribbean Cruise for two includes transportation from nearest major airport, accommodations, meals plus up to $1,000 in expense money (ARV $4,300). 3rd Grand Prize (1) a ten-day Hawaiian holiday for two includes round trip air transportation for two, hotel accommodations, sightseeing, plus up to $1,200 in spending money (ARV $7,700). All trips subject to availability and must be taken as outlined on the entry form.

4. Sweepstakes open to residents of the U.S. and Canada 18 years or older except employees and the families of Torstar Corp., its affiliates, subsidiaries and Marden-Kane, Inc. and all other agencies and persons connected with conducting this sweepstakes. All Federal, State and local laws and regulations apply. Void wherever prohibited or restricted by law. Taxes, if any are the sole responsibility of the prize winners. Canadian winners will be required to answer a skill testing question. Winners consent to the use of their name, photograph and/or likeness for publicity purposes without additional compensation.

5. For a list of prize winners, send a stamped, self-addressed envelope to Indulge A Little Sweepstakes Winners, P.O. Box 701, Sayreville, NJ 08871.

© 1989 HARLEQUIN ENTERPRISES LTD.   DL-SWPS

INDULGE A LITTLE SWEEPSTAKES

OFFICIAL RULES

SWEEPSTAKES RULES AND REGULATIONS. NO PURCHASE NECESSARY.

1. NO PURCHASE NECESSARY. To enter complete the official entry form and return with the invoice in the envelope provided. Or you may enter by printing your name, complete address and your daytime phone number on a 3 x 5 piece of paper. Include with your entry the hand printed words "Indulge A Little Sweepstakes." Mail your entry to: Indulge A Little Sweepstakes, P.O. Box 1397, Buffalo, NY 14269-1397. No mechanically reproduced entries accepted. Not responsible for late, lost, misdirected mail, or printing errors.

2. Three winners, one per month (Sept. 30, 1989, October 31, 1989 and November 30, 1989), will be selected in random drawings. All entries received prior to the drawing date will be eligible for that month's prize. This sweepstakes is under the supervision of MARDEN-KANE, INC. an independent judging organization whose decisions are final and binding. Winners will be notified by telephone and may be required to execute an affidavit of eligibility and release which must be returned within 14 days, or an alternate winner will be selected.

3. Prizes: 1st Grand Prize (1) a trip for two to Disneyworld in Orlando, Florida. Trip includes round trip air transportation, hotel accommodations for seven days and six nights, plus up to $700 expense money (ARV $3,500). 2nd Grand Prize (1) a seven-night Chandris Caribbean Cruise for two includes transportation from nearest major airport, accommodations, meals plus up to $1,000 in expense money (ARV $4,300). 3rd Grand Prize (1) a ten-day Hawaiian holiday for two includes round trip air transportation for two, hotel accommodations, sightseeing, plus up to $1,200 in spending money (ARV $7,700). All trips subject to availability and must be taken as outlined on the entry form.

4. Sweepstakes open to residents of the U.S. and Canada 18 years or older except employees and the families of Torstar Corp., its affiliates, subsidiaries and Marden-Kane, Inc. and all other agencies and persons connected with conducting this sweepstakes. All Federal, State and local laws and regulations apply. Void wherever prohibited or restricted by law. Taxes, if any are the sole responsibility of the prize winners. Canadian winners will be required to answer a skill testing question. Winners consent to the use of their name, photograph and/or likeness for publicity purposes without additional compensation.

5. For a list of prize winners, send a stamped, self-addressed envelope to Indulge A Little Sweepstakes Winners, P.O. Box 701, Sayreville, NJ 08871.

© 1989 HARLEQUIN ENTERPRISES LTD.   DL-SWPS

INDULGE A LITTLE—WIN A LOT!

Summer of '89 Subscribers-Only Sweepstakes

OFFICIAL ENTRY FORM

This entry must be received by: Sept. 30, 1989
This month's winner will be notified by: October 7, 1989
Trip must be taken between: Nov. 7, 1989–Nov. 7, 1990

YES, I want to win the Walt Disney World® vacation for two! I understand the prize includes round-trip airfare, first-class hotel, and a daily allowance as revealed on the "Wallet" scratch-off card.

Name_____

Address_____

City_____ State/Prov._____ Zip/Postal Code_____

Daytime phone number_____
　　　　　　　　　　　　Area code

Return entries with invoice in envelope provided. Each book in this shipment has two entry coupons — and the more coupons you enter, the better your chances of winning!

© 1989 HARLEQUIN ENTERPRISES LTD.

DINDL-1

INDULGE A LITTLE—WIN A LOT!

Summer of '89 Subscribers-Only Sweepstakes

OFFICIAL ENTRY FORM

This entry must be received by: Sept. 30, 1989
This month's winner will be notified by: October 7, 1989
Trip must be taken between: Nov. 7, 1989–Nov. 7, 1990

YES, I want to win the Walt Disney World® vacation for two! I understand the prize includes round-trip airfare, first-class hotel, and a daily allowance as revealed on the "Wallet" scratch-off card.

Name_____

Address_____

City_____ State/Prov._____ Zip/Postal Code_____

Daytime phone number_____
　　　　　　　　　　　　Area code

Return entries with invoice in envelope provided. Each book in this shipment has two entry coupons — and the more coupons you enter, the better your chances of winning!

© 1989 HARLEQUIN ENTERPRISES LTD.

DINDL-1